Mr Darcy's Dog Ruminates

Mr Darcy's Dog Ruminates

~ Pride & Prejudice ~
through the eyes of Julius Caesar, Darcy's dog

by Y. M. Whitehead

Copyright © 2014 by Y. M. Whitehead

All rights reserved.
No part of this book may be reproduced, distributed,
or transmitted in any form or by any means,
without express written permission from the author,
except in the case of quotations by a reviewer.

This book is a work of fiction.
Names, characters, and incidents portrayed in it
are products of the author's imaginations,
and any resemblance to actual persons, living or otherwise,
event or locations is entirely coincidental.

To Jane Austen,
who gave us the wealth of 'Pride and Prejudice'.

Table of Contents

The List of Characters

(The Darcy Connection)

Mr Fitzwilliam Darcy (of Pemberley, Derbyshire) – the hero, a very wealthy landowner of a vast estate, income of ten thousand a year, gives the first impression of being very arrogant

Miss Georgiana Darcy – Mr Darcy's younger sister

Mr Trent – Mr Darcy's valet

Julius Caesar – Mr Darcy's dog, the narrator of the book

Mr Wickham – a Militia officer, a cad, the son of Mr Darcy's late father's steward

Colonel Fitzwilliam – Mr Darcy's cousin

Lady Catherine de Bourgh (of Rosings Park, Kent) – Mr Darcy, Georgiana Darcy, and Colonel Fitzwilliam's aunt, Mr Collins's patroness, a bit of a tartar

Mrs Younge – Miss Darcy's former companion, a dubious character

(The Bennet Connection)

Mr Bennet (of Longbourn, Hertfordshire), a country gentleman, income of two thousand a year

Mrs Bennet – Mr Bennet's wife, the mother of five daughters, a voluble and silly woman

Miss Jane Bennet – the eldest daughter, very beautiful and of sweet nature

Miss Elizabeth Bennet (Lizzy) – the heroine, the second daughter, beautiful, feisty and intelligent

Miss Mary Bennet – the third daughter, not exactly a barrel of laughs, the least beautiful of the sisters

Miss Catherine Bennet (Kitty) – the fourth daughter, a bit of an airhead

Miss Lydia Bennet – the fifth daughter, a complete airhead

Mr Collins (of Hunsford, Kent) – a clergyman, Mr Bennet's distant cousin to whom the Longbourn estate is entailed, a complete buffoon

Mr Gardiner (of Cheapside, London) – Mrs Bennet's younger brother, who is in trade

Mrs Gardiner – Mr Gardiner's wife

(The Bingley Connection)

Mr Charles Bingley (of Netherfield Park, Hertfordshire) – Darcy's best friend, the tenant of Netherfield Park, rich and agreeable, income of five thousand a year

Miss Caroline Bingley – Mr Bingley's younger sister, has set her sights on Mr Darcy

Mrs Louisa Hurst – Mr Bingley's older sister (married)

Mr Hurst (of Grosvenor Street, London) – Mr Bingley's brother-in-law

(The Lucases)

Sir William Lucas (of Lucas Lodge, Hertfordshire) – the Bennets' family friend and neighbour

Miss Charlotte Lucas – the eldest daughter, Miss Elizabeth Bennet's close friend

Miss Maria Lucas – Miss Lucas's younger sister

Dixon – Miss Lucas's dog

Chapter 1

In which I shall introduce myself and my revered master, if I may

It is a truth very little acknowledged that we dogs have a very good understanding of human language and everything that is going on in the human world. This truth is so little known that human beings have no inhibitions whatsoever in front of us and bare their most intimate thoughts to us.

I am a dog, of the breed 'English Setter', and I answer to the name of 'Julius Caesar'. I am truly fond of the name, in fact, even fonder of it than the name, Augustus, which many dogs consider is out and out the most ripping name for a dog that one could ever think of. Which incidentally is the name given to one of my brothers.

I am no ordinary dog, my pedigree, although I hate to boast, is very good. My great-great-great grandfather in fact worked under his Majesty, before his Majesty lost his marbles.

I was born in the kennel belonging to my master when God was pleased to send me to this world three and a half years ago, ergo, I am just approaching the prime of life. As you might have become cognisant, I am exceptionally well endowed with intelligence for an animal, which fact I humbly say I greatly owe to my master.

My master is Mr Fitzwilliam Darcy of Pemberley, which is a superfine estate in Derbyshire. He is a very powerful man and exceedingly clever. So much so that he is even capable of conversing with me, a creature of an entirely different species. Or ... perhaps, if I might be bold, I could say that I am the cleverer party as my good master probably talks to me without realizing that I understand everything. No humans seem to be truly aware of the degree of intelligence that we dogs possess. We are intrinsically far, far better blessed than any other species with good understanding of the complicated modus operandi of the world of the human species.

I was born of Claudius and Octavia, who, despite their autumn years, both still serve under Mr Darcy with me alongside all my siblings and cousins, who without a single exception have been named after Roman emperors and empresses. But if I might just draw your attention to a trivial fact, I am the only one honoured with the surname, 'Caesar'.

My parents, who also served my master's honoured father, tell me that old Mr Darcy was as great a master as any dog or any human alike would have boasted of serving under, and the present master will be just the same, possibly to an even greater degree. According to my parents, when old Mr Darcy suddenly departed from this world five years ago, my master, notwithstanding his youthful years, bravely took over the standardbearership of the great Darcy clan, and has shown a greatness, an astuteness and a flair which promise in time to be even more illustrious than his father's.

My earliest recollection of my master was some fortnight after I was born, when my master was so condescending as to come and grace the kennel with his august presence and as to inquire how my mother, my siblings and I were faring.

“I wish to have one of these young fellows reared to be my especial companion,” said my revered master to Mr Jerome, the master of hounds, “as well as to be serviceable for fowling alongside others.

Which fellow would you recommend to me, Jerome?"

"This puppy here is already showing great signs of intelligence and energy," observed Mr Jerome, indicating me, to my subsequent great happiness, "to say nothing of such friendliness and gentleness as all English Setters are renowned for."

Thus, my master was pleased to settle for me, and the next moment, I was lifted up by warm, large and gentle hands, then cradled in most comfortable arms, enveloped in the heavenly scent of musk which emanated from my master's superbly tailored coat, and I found myself peering up into my master's handsome patrician face.

"You are indeed an intelligent looking fellow," my master was kind enough to say to me in his beautiful baritone. "I like your face. It shows something of good-nature and mischievousness as well as intelligence, which I find most congenial."

* * * * *

So, this is the manner in which I became my master's companion, 'highly esteemed' companion, if I may say so myself.

During these three and a half years since that first encounter, I have come to know my master very intimately. He is a man of few words and by and large a solitary man. I have seldom heard him laugh, though I have occasionally seen on his handsome profile a faint smile which could be described as 'wry'. If I were to select a word from my lexicon to best describe his look and mien, I would choose the word 'unapproachable'. However, once he forms close friendship with people, they invariably pledge staunch and determined loyalty to him as well as he to them. My master is a man of honour whose word is his bond, and people place whole-hearted trust in him.

But as I have already mentioned, my master is not a man of many words, and he very seldom divulges his own affairs to others, to wit, he is never one to open his own heart to others easily. However, even a stoical, seemingly self-sufficient gentleman of my master's ilk needs someone on occasions to confide in, wherein I come.

My master often confides in me, this humble quadruped, imparting his innermost thoughts, which he would not do to anyone belonging to the highest echelon of all species, by which I mean 'human beings'. Maybe, my master maintains a notion that I do not have the faintest clue what he is saying, or even if he ever suspects that I do understand something, the fact that I possess no verbal means of communication with his fellow human beings can set his mind at rest and allows him to unburthen his heart to me freely.

For example, when, at the beginning of July just gone, my master discovered that Miss Darcy, his beloved sister younger than him by more than two lustra, suffered a minor aberration from her paths of rectitude and was nearly cozened into eloping with Mr Wickham, a black-hearted blighter, I was the one to whom my master unburdened his angst.

“Alas, Julius Caesar, my dear old boy,” he said to me, “I have always known Wickham to be a man with a nature most putrid and corrupt, and yet never expected him to have the gall to prey upon Georgiana! I have a good mind to call that villain out!”

When my master thus lamented in an unusually raised, anguished tone of voice, I felt, in spite of myself, not a little panicked, fearful that he might really go and slap a glove across Mr Wickham's face and take that most unwise, wholly unrecommmendable path, viz, demand a duel of that most unworthy gentleman, although I shortly reminded myself that my master was not so reckless a person as to be carried away by a momentary ire and suffer a lifetime of regret.

I have heard through a highly dependable grapevine that my master is considered to be one of the dearest darlings of the *ton* despite the fact that he is also reckoned to be the coldest fish of the *ton* at the same time. People often seem to say that at public gatherings such as balls, my master sweeps his eyes over the throng with distant, aloof gaze. But in my humble opinion, to call him cold because of that would not be an accurate assessment. It is more like he is searching for something, or rather, searching for someone, a soul-mate.

My beloved master, in truth, is a warm and caring gentleman

notwithstanding his outward aloof impression, which people often describe as 'like an ice statue'. But his trouble is that he has no flair for small talk, nor has he any inclination to cure himself of that deficiency. It is not that he considers the art of exchanging pleasantry not worth cultivating, or endeavouring to attain it below his dignity. It is merely because he does not feel the pressing necessity for it at the present moment. What he needs is to fall in love with some lady who has plenty of it, and to feel the desire to learn the skill to converse with her. To feel the need is the shortest and surest way to attaining anything. As they often say, necessity is the mother of invention.

I do not believe my master has ever been truly in love. A real love in which two people's souls are joined and even just calling the other's name would tug at one's heartstrings. He does not know what it is like to love, to unreservedly care for someone, till one craves to know and find out everything about the person one loves. And until he does, until he finds what being in love is in reality, he will not understand the beauty of conversing in a true exchange of two minds.

Chapter 2

In which I shall introduce my master's friends in Hertfordshire

A young gentleman by the name of Mr Charles Bingley has been my master's most cherished friend for the last three years. I recollect that I was a puppy-faced six-month-old when my master met Mr Bingley for the first time. He was a gentleman yet to reach his nineteenth year then with a visage of unparalleled amiableness and a bearing of uncommon agreeableness. I sensed that my master took an almost instant liking to the young gentleman, which was indeed such an atypical thing for him, who was normally so overly circumspect in forming friendship as to make even me, a mere humble canine companion, feel not a little impatient.

Now, Mr Bingley is just at this moment with my master here in my master's London residence. According to what I have gathered from their conversation, Mr Bingley has attained the lease for a country estate in Hertfordshire, which is called Netherfield Park, and, as I understand, has already taken up residence there.

Thus, having come from the afore-mentioned estate for a brief visit, Mr Bingley is busy extolling to my master many aspects of the estate.

"So you have found Netherfield Park entirely to your liking, then?" my master says to Mr Bingley.

"Darcy, my good man!" cries Mr Bingley excitedly, with his amicable face absolutely a-beaming. "It well exceeds the most sanguine of my expectations! Absolutely bang-up!"

Mr Bingley, who is forever happy to take things as they come, is the most happy-go-lucky, devil-may-care sort of individual that I have ever had the honour of knowing and, as I secretly assess, 'the most sanguine of his expectations', or 'bang-up' – whatever it means – might not amount to much. My master seems to be of the same opinion.

"I am happy to hear it, Bingley," says my master, "though I am so well acquainted with your easy-going nature that I fear you will declare it to be 'bang-up' even if it is a most wretched, beleaguered place, surrounded by boorish neighbours."

"Darcy, I know I am not as fastidious as you are, but even I can tell the difference between a bang-up place and a beleaguered one!" protests Mr Bingley. "I aver, it really is frightfully spiffing!"

My master is serious, fastidious and circumspect, a kind of gentleman who would plan about ten moves ahead before he takes action, whereas Mr Bingley is very much a gentleman with a decided tendency to act upon impulse. Their natures are as polar opposite as polar opposite can ever come. I often think it a great pity that one could not mix the natures of those two gentlemen, stir the mixture up thoroughly, and divide it in two. The result product would be perfect.

Not that I have anything against my master's disposition. Indeed, never have I seen a young gentleman anywhere who is finer or more impressive than my master, but it is my humble opinion that if my master could learn to let his guard down a little, to let himself be less awe-inspiring and intimidating, he would be even more perfect.

Mr Bingley wishes my master to visit Netherfield, and is making an earnest appeal to gain that end.

"Darcy, say you will come! I will not accept any answer but Yes! I promise you, you shall have as capital a time as no other. Fine balls, dinners and social gatherings, you shall have aplenty. Oh, and furthermore, a multitude of exceptionally pretty young ladies – or at least that is what I have been told! They say that that part of Hertfordshire abounds in beauties!"

Balls, dinner parties and social gatherings ... these are hardly the things that could entice my master.

My master is what one calls 'an asocial' and detests social occasions. And as for pretty young ladies, well, the mention of whom should make normal young gentlemen excited and willing, but the problem is that my master is far from a typical young gentleman. His high standing in society, his wealth, and his noble and handsome mien with his impressive stature, have all combined to make him one of the most sought-after of the *ton*, and wherever he goes, he is in peril of being mobbed as a matrimonial prize. As a result, the mention of a multitude of young ladies would have a contrary effect, and be more likely to make him recoil.

However, my master is always very indulgent to Mr Bingley, and if there is one thing my master wishes to avoid, it is to disappoint Mr Bingley. So he acquiesces albeit grudgingly with his characteristic wry smile.

* * * * *

Now I am at Netherfield Park with my master, having arrived here late yesterday evening.

It is a fine estate, though not as fine as Pemberley. But of course, one would have to traverse far to happen across an estate as impressive as Pemberley, and I am not saying so as an idle blind vaunt just because it belongs to my master and I wish its glory to rub off onto me. Whenever my fellow canines accompany their masters on a visit to Pemberley, they are invariably most voluble in their laudatory utterances for Pemberley.

Netherfield Park reposes in a tranquil idyll of north Hertfordshire not very far from Baldock. The easy distance to Town in which the estate is situated seems to have met the hearty approval of Mr Bingley's two sisters, Mrs Hurst, the elder, and Miss Bingley, the younger, who, if I might be allowed to venture upon an opinion, are devilish difficult ladies to please upon any issue, as they are the type of ladies who would find enormous pleasures in nitpicking.

I am not very fond of them, and that is rather putting it mildly. If I may be more honest, I detest them enormously. Neither of them possess any of the amiableness and the jollity, which are salient features of their brother's nature. It is hard to believe they have the same blood flowing in their veins as his. Their facial expressions are perpetually scowling as if they had just swallowed something awfully sour and disgusting, and their demeanour is constantly haughty and disdainful except when they are fawning over whomsoever they deem their betters. Especially to my master, their attitude could only be described as 'toad-eater-ish' if there is such a word.

As for their attitude towards me, it would be most aptly defined as 'two-faced', as they treat me as if sugar wouldn't melt in their mouth in front of my master, fussing over me saying what a fine specimen of a dog I am and how they adore me and all that, but behind his back, they ignore me at best, which I do not mind, but more often than not, they are rather short and rough with me, which I do mind. They certainly are not animal lovers and I have this firm conviction that there seldom are nice people among animal haters.

* * * * *

Now, this Miss Bingley, I have a very good reason to believe, has her eye firmly set upon my master. My master is rather tantalizingly, or sometimes even 'teeth-gnashingly' slow at cottoning on to matters of this nature, and has not much notion of what danger he might find himself in.

That is the trouble with intelligent men. They seem to place too much reliance upon their own wisdom and intelligence, and have a decided tendency to consider female intelligence inferior to that of men and to grossly underestimate female cunning. Indeed, how many times have I had to rescue my master from situations which might have put him at 'point non plus' concerning Miss Bingley? The said lady is awfully cunning and calculating, and time and time again, endeavours to be alone with my master, or at times even dares to scheme to contrive a situation in which my master might have seemingly compromised her.

For example, only this morning, when I was dozing contentedly in the tranquil quiet of the library, kneeling at my master's feet while my master sat in one of the wing-chairs perusing today's Times, Miss Bingley sailed into the room.

“Oh, Mr Darcy!” cried she and pressed her palm to her chest, feigning to be utterly taken by surprise to find my master there. As if she had not known! Who was she trying to deceive?! I almost snorted. Instead of taking care to leave the library door open as a normal young lady with any decorum would certainly have done, she, who had her own ulterior motive, closed it craftily but firmly behind her clearly for the purpose of shutting herself up with my master in the room.

I would not have any of that. I ran to the door with utmost celerity, and by turning the knob with my muzzle and paw, I opened the door, which feat I had long since learned to perform to perfection, and left it as wide open as possible. It is indeed truly fortunate that none of the principal rooms here in Netherfield have locks, as locking and unlocking are the arts which I have not managed to master owing to the awkwardness of my paws. Well, in any event, I then ran back to stand beside my master like a celebrated sentinel. My auditory perception, which is zillion times more acute than my master's, caught the sound of Miss Bingley's clicking her tongue as if she was seriously displeased, and my visual anatomical organs which also are far sharper than my master's saw her frown down at me awfully, albeit covertly, as obviously she did not wish my master to hear or see her do so.

* * * * *

Chapter 2

And at this present moment, as my master has come outside to take a peaceful afternoon stroll with me, Miss Bingley also has come abroad, indefatigably pursuing my master.

"Why, Mr Darcy! How fortuitously we have met!" Miss Bingley lets out a cry, yet again feigning to have been surprised to find my master as if she had not expected it at all. "I, too, have come to take a turn in the park. What a happy coincidence!" she adds, though she well knows herself that there is nothing coincidental about her being there! "How pleasant it is to walk under the celestial blue!" she almost coos.

I know Miss Bingley desperately hopes to take my master's arm, so, whenever I see the danger of her trying to come to stand next to my master, I cleverly intercede by coming in between my master and her in a most nonchalant manner. I will not let her have her own way.

It is a battle of wits, Miss Bingley's and mine. But I know perfectly well that I am at a decided advantage, as Miss Bingley has no notion whatsoever of the extent of my intellectual endowment. In her eyes, I am but a canine companion with no intelligence or cunning.

In this fashion, I have to keep a constant and close vigil so that Miss Bingley would not succeed in her schemes. Indeed, I would never wish to leave my master's side for fear of Miss Bingley's pouncing upon my master and getting the better of him.

Chapter 2

Chapter 3

In which my master meets a lady with ripe lips with rather saucy curves

There is going to be an assembly ball in the nearby town called Meryton this evening.

Formal gatherings such as balls and dinner parties are out of bounds for such as I, and whither, however much I wish to, I am not allowed to accompany my master. But there will be so many people about and my master will be surrounded by a teeming crowd at all times during such an event. However desperate or brazen she might be, Miss Bingley is not likely to take any drastic measures for fear of making herself look indecorous or ridiculous, when she wishes to cut a fine figure in front of new people. So, I see no danger to fear on my master's account from that quarter.

* * * * *

Now it is past midnight, and my master has just returned from the assembly ball in Meryton.

As I have predicted, he does not appear to have drawn much enjoyment from attending the ball.

“It was a deuced tedious ball as I had fully anticipated,” my master talks to me as it is his routine practice after such events, musing upon what went on at the assembly ball, “though Bingley was up in the seventh heaven as he succeeded in having a girl of his dreams stand up with him for two sets of dances. She was indeed an uncommonly handsome girl, although a little too timid and quiet-looking for my liking, if not to say insipid, despite her spun-gold hair. I prefer someone with a little more striking, strong features, with vivacity and intelligent looks. I was forced to dance two sets, one with Mrs Hurst and the other with Miss Bingley, which I considered more than I could tolerate for one night's ordeal.”

So, my master danced with Miss Bingley again. I thought as much. Oh, why, why does he not understand that it is not wise to give Miss Bingley any cause for hope? He should not have done so. It is far better to shun her at all times. Why does he think I am always so assiduous in thwarting Miss Bingley?

“Bingley as usual was full of censure for my fastidiousness,” my master continues to muse, paying no heed or attention to the worries I endure on his account, “and endeavoured to have me dance with the sister of the said handsome girl of his dreams, but of course, to no avail. I concede, however, that this sister did have a little more character in her face, with dark sparking eyes full of expression and ripe lips with rather saucy curves, but for all that, she was not handsome enough for me to be prevailed upon to dance with.”

It is a very rare thing for my master to talk of a lady's eyes, let alone her lips, 'ripe' at that! Notwithstanding his censure, this lady seems to have left some impression upon my master's heart which is as yet to be seriously touched, although he himself does not even seem to realize it.

* * * * *

There have been several social gatherings in the neighbourhood since we came to Netherfield, and earnestly entreated by Mr Bingley, my master has attended all of them though not without a few grumbles.

As I have already mentioned, I am not granted permission to be present at those events, so I have to be satisfied to trust my master's own circumspection and common-sense to guide him and succour him at those precarious times and help him come out whole and safe from Miss Bingley's clutches without my protection.

Since that Meryton assembly, judging from what little he has dropped in my hearing, it appears to me that my master, though by almost imperceptible degrees, has become more conscious of that lady whose 'ripe lips' he talked of, that is, the sister of the lady whom Mr Bingley was quite taken by. But I do not think that any humans would have noticed this very subtle change in my master, my master himself included.

According to the jigsaw pieces of information I have so far been able to gather, they are Misses Bennets of Longbourn. Mr Bingley's choice seems to be the eldest of five sisters, Miss Jane Bennet, and the lady whom my master is unusually taken by is the second eldest, Miss Elizabeth Bennet.

These two gentlemen's attitudes concerning their own growing attraction to the respective ladies are widely different. Mr Bingley without reserve talks of Miss Bennet in anyone's presence with much animation, perpetually extolling the lady's every single aspect as one incomparable. Whereas my master never mentions Miss Elizabeth to anyone. So, no one has even the smallest inkling so far of my master's growing interest in Miss Elizabeth.

Even to me, my master only mentions Miss Elizabeth cursorily, and never actually dwells upon her long.

But we dogs are very intuitive. In fact, one could say that we dogs possess some special instinct or intuition handed down through generations since the dawn of history, when all God's creatures, even including humans, were far more attuned to nature and nearer to God. If I dare venture my humble opinion, humans have, during the aeon-long process of their development, which they call 'evolution', gradually lost this intuitive faculty that some other species still possess. And as for this matter of possessing intuitive faculty, I say without vaunt that dogs are at the very apogee of all species.

And we dogs have an acute sense of smell as well, which could also be defined to be as intuitive as it is sensory. When my master mentions Miss Elizabeth's name, my acute olfactory sense can detect that something, some especial chemical no doubt, is released from my master's person ... presumably some substance similar to that which we animals give off when we are sexually stimulated. Nothing can be a surer sign that my master is beginning to be very interested in the lady.

* * * * *

Now, there is to be a dinner party at Netherfield this evening, and many a prominent family in the neighbourhood is invited.

As I have already referred to, my master frequently mentions Miss Elizabeth's name to me, in such a way as he has never mentioned any other lady's name before, which has come firmly to convince me that my master's interest in her is growing stronger and stronger apace. So, I have been all agog to make her acquaintance, but so far have been unable to achieve that end.

So, I dearly hope I shall be able to do so tonight, as I know for a fact that all the Bennets are invited. But I am well aware that the chances of my being admitted to such a formal gathering, even if it is held at Netherfield, is very slim. All the same, I am hoping to catch sight of the lady at least.

The guests are arriving, and I make myself as unobtrusive as possible while I sit in the far dark corner of the front hall surveying the people arriving and hoping to learn which of the young ladies is Miss Elizabeth.

A young lady who has just arrived happens to cast her eyes my way and sees me. She lets out a small cry of joy and trips up to me. I cannot greet her with a loud woof as I do not wish to attract too much attention to myself, but I eagerly hold out one forepaw to her, then the other in greeting, to show my heart-felt welcome. She, with apparent fondness, takes my offered paws laughingly, then stroking me with hands tender, warm and loving, says,

"Oh, you are a beautiful creature! To whom do you belong?"

She stays with me caressing and hugging me for a few moments in a most affectionate manner, which would touch any dog's ego and turn any dog's head. At the end of which, however, she says heaving a long, regretful sigh,

"I am afraid I must go. I would much rather stay with you here, but needs must. I had better hurry before I am dragged to the drawing room by the scruff and make a spectacle of myself." And she walks away with a few regretful backward glances.

The dinner party has finished and the guests are gone, and now the Netherfield people are gathered in the drawing room, talking about the dinner party, or to be more precise, delivering verdicts upon the populace.

The comments Miss Bingley and Mrs Hurst make are as expected rather scathing. Of course, they very seldom have anything remotely complimentary to say about anyone, that is, if not about my master.

Mr Bingley is as usual voluble in extolling Miss Bennet's beauty in both her person and character.

Then, "By the by, there are many who talk of Miss Eliza Bennet as one of the most reputed beauties of these parts," says Miss Bingley suddenly. I look sharp at my master, but as anticipated, his expression does not change even an infinitesimal degree.

"She, a beauty? I should as soon call her mother a wit," my master drawls in a most uninterested voice.

I concede that it is a good ploy to feign total absence of interest in that quarter in front of Miss Bingley, but it sometimes amazes me how well humans are able to disguise their feelings where love is concerned. We canines are far less skilled at hiding things of that nature. When we are interested in someone, or rather in some dog, we cannot help showing our partiality so openly and unequivocally that there is absolutely no disguising the fact.

To my regret, I have not been able to ascertain which of the young ladies was Miss Elizabeth. The young lady who came to me in the front hall had such beautiful eyes and such an engaging manner. Could she have been Miss Elizabeth? Oh, I dearly, dearly hope so!

I will heartily approve of my master's good taste in women, if indeed that lady turns out to be Miss Elizabeth!

* * * * *

I have a bad, bad premonition. Miss Bingley, if she were to have any inkling that my master has begun to view a lady other than herself with an unprecedented interest with or without his own awareness, would become even more desperate and her hot pursuit of my master would become even hotter.

Chapter 3

Chapter 4

In which there arises an occasion that necessitates the two eldest Misses Bennets' staying at Netherfield

Mr Bingley's sisters have formed some sort of friendship with Miss Bennet, although, judging from their demeanour towards the lady, I rather suspect that they regard the relationship more of condescension and charity on their part than reciprocal friendship.

They seem to have invited the said lady to Netherfield to have dinner with them today. The gentlemen (my master, Mr Bingley and Mr Hurst – Mr Bingley's brother-in-law) have gone abroad to dine with the officers of the regiment stationed in the town of Meryton. Mr Bingley will be furious that they have kept it a secret from him when he hears about it when he comes back.

I have not been allowed to accompany my master, but am quite content to be left at home, fully aware that there is no danger to assail my master as Miss Bingley will not be able to chase after him, either.

Now I look outside and notice that the sky which I thought was cheerily blue only a few moments ago has turned completely slate grey and rain is pouring down in great sheets.

Miss Bennet has just arrived. Oh, dear! She is soaked to the skin! She must have met the heavy rain upon the way.

"Good gracious!" Mrs Hurst cries out. "Jane, dear, you look an image of a drowned rat!" thus she uses a somewhat uncomplimentary metaphor. "Have you not come in the carriage!?"

They show Miss Bennet to a guest chamber so that, I presume, she could be rid of her soaked clothing and borrow one of the sisters' dresses.

"I am very sorry to put you to so much trouble," says Miss Bennet. She must be feeling very cold, as her teeth are chattering. "Papa needed the horses on the farm, so I came upon my nag."

"Oh, Jane, Jane, poor dear," says Miss Bingley, "it must be awful not to be able to afford as many horses as you wish!"

They have finished dinner, and are now relaxing in the drawing room. The rain is still cascading down, and Mr Bingley's sisters have invited Miss Bennet to stay, which she has accepted thankfully.

I am certain Miss Bennet has caught a chill as a result of getting soaked. She appears awfully flushed and poorly.

I wonder at the insensitivity of the two sisters, who do not seem to realize or indeed care about the wretched condition Miss Bennet clearly is in. They just talk and talk about themselves, which is mostly self-praises, or else ask Miss Bennet some questions about her and her family which are brazenly probing and impertinent. Miss Bennet bravely endures their endless tattle despite her worsening condition.

Insensitive as they are, the two ladies come to realize by and by that something is amiss with Miss Bennet. They volubly inquire what the matter is with her, which takes another deuced long time, during which Miss Bennet is yet longer obliged to suffer in silence ...

But, thank god, they at very long last seem to have decided it is about time they put her to bed.

The gentlemen have just returned, and have been notified of Miss

Bennet's being obliged to remain at Netherfield because of her chill.

"So, you were going to invite Miss Bennet to dinner!" cries Mr Bingley. "Why did you not tell me, Louisa, and you, Caroline!? Had I known, I would not have gone to the dinner with the officers! Moreover, I could have sent a carriage to fetch her, and then, she would not have caught a chill!"

"Bingley, you could not have cried off the prior engagement with the officers for such a reason," says my master. "That would have been most irresponsible."

"Well, I suppose you are right. But I am still put out that they did not tell me. That has always been the case with them. They always try to keep anything a secret which might be of interest to me for some contrary reason of their own!"

"Well, try not to allow yourself to be worked up over this, Bingley. Just consider. If you had known, you would have sent a carriage for Miss Bennet, and if Miss Bennet had come in the carriage, she would not have caught a chill, and if she had not caught a chill, she would have gone home after dinner. Look on the brighter side."

Mr Bingley seems suddenly to remember that the lady of his heart is under his own roof, and looks the picture of happiness.

"Yes, when I think of it in that way, it is exactly as you say, is it not!? Well, I think I should forgive my sisters, then."

* * * * *

This morning has found Miss Bennet worse, and Mr Bingley has reached the height of elation. Not that he is elated by the fact that she is more poorly. Oh, no, of course not! He is all anxiety and concern for her condition and all solicitude and attention for her comfort, but Miss Bennet's condition will inevitably necessitate her to remain at Netherfield for sometime, and the fond heart of the gentleman is suffused with the happiness of having the lady in his house at least for some foreseeable future.

Miss Bennet seems to have dispatched a missive home, telling her family of her condition.

Chapter 4

* * * * *

As I now wander about the park alone while the ladies and the gentlemen are breaking the fast, I espy a lady walking up to the house at a brisk pace. A little closer scrutiny reveals that it is the lady who came up to greet me in the front hall on the day of the Netherfield dinner party. I have met her only once, and that only very briefly. But I recognise her perfectly. We, English Setters, are renowned for our ability to remember people, but even among us, I have obtained great kudos for being exceptionally good with people's faces, so good that I often astound everybody when I immediately know someone even if I have seen him only once very briefly, or haven't seen him in a very long while.

Now, when I observe the lady closely as she comes up to where I stand, I see that her overall impression is sprightly and energetic rather than elegant. But I like that vivacity of hers. And her face is indeed so lovely as well as friendly and good-natured, that it is far cry from Miss Bingley's and Mrs Hurst's, which I always find are awfully pinched and sour.

It is hard to believe that this lady's lovely face and Mr Bingley's sisters' obnoxious faces could belong to the same species.

I perceive that the lady has just noticed my presence. She gives out a small cry of joy as she did on that former occasion, and runs towards me. She seems to be truly fond of dogs.

“Good morrow, Julius Caesar! Am I not right? That is your name, is it not?” says she, with a friendly, genial pat upon my back. “And you are Mr Darcy's trusted companion?”

I now have this happy conviction that this lady must be one of the Misses Bennets. Why would the lady have come here otherwise than to enquire after her sick sister? And something tells me that she is no other than the second sister, Miss Elizabeth, as it can easily be assumed that the second eldest is the one closest to the eldest.

To show my hearty welcome, I vigorously wag my tail, to the extent that people might fear it might snap off, which degree of wholehearted reception I never vouchsafe on either of Mr Bingley's sisters. To them I wag my tail less than half-heartedly if at all, and that, only when it is absolutely imperative.

"Oh, what a friendly, lovable creature you are! So obliging! So welcoming!" continues she, hugging me in that playful and loving fashion of the former occasion, which is most congenial to me. "So different from your haughty master!" she adds.

So different from my haughty master!? Now, now, what has my master gone and done this time to elicit such a remark from this lady?

The trouble with my master is, I ponder with a sigh, that regardless of time and place, and not heeding to whom, he acts as if he did not care a damn about other people. It all comes, not from his sense of superiority or disregard for other people's feelings, but precisely to the contrary, from his sense of profound unease and shyness in the presence of others.

He is like a swan whose outward appearance gives the impression that he glides without effort with majestic calm on the water-surface, and yet whose feet are frantically kicking underneath where the human eye does not see. But no one seems to understand that fact. No one has ever noticed it. No one can see my master's true nature, the sensitivity and the bashfulness behind his severely aloof façade.

"I am Lizzy. I am come to inquire how my sister is faring," says she when we have done with greeting, to confirm my belief to my great happiness that she is indeed Miss Elizabeth, and I secretly congratulate my master on his excellent choice of women. "Will you show me the way?" Miss Elizabeth adds.

Miss Elizabeth is just like my master. She talks to me as if she thought I understand everything.

I head the way, and we come to the front door. I bark vigorously to alert Mr Bingley's butler, whose name escapes me. Bates or Bains, or something or other.

Miss Elizabeth repeats the same thing to the butler. "I am Miss Elizabeth Bennet. I am come to inquire how my sister, Miss Bennet, is faring."

Miss Elizabeth is shown into the family reception room, where the ladies and gentlemen are now gathered after breakfast, and I happen to glance over to Miss Bingley and catch the moment in which her gaze flips over towards my master in a furtive but intensely searching manner. Seeing my master gazing at Miss Elizabeth, she bites her lower lip as if she were seriously vexed. Then, I immediately know that Miss Bingley already entertains a tangible suspicion of my master's dawning attraction to Miss Elizabeth.

Has my master let slip some observation or given a look which has given rise to Miss Bingley's suspicion?

The trouble with my master is that he is very careless about that kind of thing, despite the fact that he is fundamentally an almost excessively circumspect man. He thinks that females are all like males, who are intrinsically the infinitely simpler gender whose guileless make-up would make them view things in an uncomplicated, straightforward fashion without guise. Men usually say one thing, and mean one thing, whereas women often say one thing, and mean another, sometimes even the complete opposite. Of course, even my master can occasionally be deceptive, but the ability to deceive in females is far, far greater.

That characteristic is universal. It does not apply to human females alone. Canines are exactly the same. My father often grumbles about the complicated manner in which my mother's mind seems to operate. And I believe it applies to other animals, too, to almost the same degree.

* * * * *

Miss Elizabeth seems to have been invited to stay at Netherfield to keep her sick sister company till she is better.

What must it have cost Miss Bingley to be compelled to tender that invitation to Miss Elizabeth? It must have been quite a sight to see her begrudgingly offer the invitation. Oh, how I wish I had seen it!

Chapter 4

* * * * *

Now, dinner finished, Miss Elizabeth has excused herself and left the others, to be with her ailing sister again, and Miss Bingley has opened a vicious attack upon Miss Elizabeth. Her indecorum in coming to Netherfield, so early this morning and moreover unchaperoned, is long dwelt on. Her wild appearance on that occasion after tramping along in all that mud and mire also is harped upon.

She persists on and on ... and on ... and on. The list is endless.

And then, "I am afraid, Mr Darcy, that this adventure has rather affected your admiration of Miss Elizabeth's fine eyes," delivers Miss Bingley with undisguised sardonicism.

Hidden behind the disdain which Miss Bingley apparently wishes others to believe is no more than that, I detect a distinct trace of another emotion – jealousy.

My master must have said something to Miss Bingley about the fineness of Miss Elizabeth's eyes. He should have been more guarded.

And then, to make the matter even worse, my master says as a reply to Miss Bingley's comment,

"Not at all. They were brightened by the exercise."

I almost let out a groan. It was most unwise. Now, Miss Bingley is certain to raise her assiduity in pursuing my master to a staggering level.

Miss Bingley without a rival is bad enough, but Miss Bingley with a threat of a rival's emergence is a frightful thought indeed.

Chapter 4

Chapter 5

In which I meet Mrs Bennet and her two youngest daughters

I am come out to have a little run around the grounds, when I espy a carriage approaching the house. Three female faces are seen pressed against the carriage windows. I know their faces. I am sure I have seen them before, but I do not know their names. I can easily guess, however, that they are Mrs Bennet and her daughters, who must have come to see how Miss Bennet is faring.

I see the two young ladies pushing and shoving each other in rather a puerile and boisterous manner, apparently vying to decide who gets to see out of the window.

As I said, I have come out wholly intending to indulge myself in a pleasant constitutional run, but my inquisitiveness gets the better of me, and I follow the carriage back to the house.

In front of the house, the carriage halts, and thence the ladies emerge, the young ladies still in contention, apparently this time about who gets to get out of the carriage first.

"Oh, fie, Kitty, fie, Lydia!" their mother remonstrates fretfully. "Do stop fighting each other so! Spare more thought for your poor mother,

I beg you! You do not know how frazzled my nerves are! But lo! What a fine façade! Every time I see it, it takes my breath away! So grand! So tasteful! Sir William Lucas's is nothing compared with this, nor is Mr Robinson's, nor indeed is Mr Watson's! Jane will certainly be the happiest and grandest of all girls around here when she becomes the mistress of Netherfield! And I shall be the very envy of all the mamas! What a delightful thought it is indeed!"

I feel like rolling my eyeballs heavenwards. If this lady is their mother and these young ladies their sisters, Miss Bennet and Miss Elizabeth have a great deal indeed to be pitied for!

The two young ladies, having noticed my presence, let out loud, rapturous cries, which makes me jump almost out of my skin. Like Miss Elizabeth, they, too, must be fond of dogs, which I acknowledge is a very good thing, and I am gratified with that, but unlike Miss Elizabeth, whose joy at seeing me is usually a little more controlled, they rush to me in clamorous elation, which staggers me not a little and makes me step back a pace. And also unlike Miss Elizabeth, who hugs me in tender, warm caresses, they squeeze me till I am almost out of breath, and ruffle my fur vigorously, paying no respect to my dignity, until my normally tidy hair is completely tousled, which I am sure has made me look rather silly.

Having messed up my fur to their hearts' content in this wise, they trip back to their mother, who is still standing there admiring the façade in a most satisfied manner as if Netherfield were already safely and firmly in the bag.

Presently, the butler, Mr Bateman, as I now remember is his name, opens the door in answer to the lady's summons, and I find they indeed are the Bennets.

They are ushered into the drawing room, where my master, Mr Bingley, Miss Bingley, and the Hursts are gathered. Mr Bingley receives them with his characteristic good-naturedness, and Miss Bingley, with her customary superciliousness.

"Why! I cannot thank you enough for your great kindness to my poor suffering daughter, Jane! Indeed I cannot! When it began raining heavily after Jane left yesterday, it worried me awfully, but as soon as I was reminded that it was here, for Netherfield, she was heading and how very kind and caring you always are to her, I knew my worries were totally unnecessary! Indeed I did! Who else could boast of being blessed with such friends! Jane is the luckiest girl in the kingdom! Indeed she is!" Mrs Bennet thus greets them with a torrent of speech.

I can see that Mrs Bennet's vulgarity is a heavy strain on my master, who holds anything vulgar in abhorrence.

I can hear Mrs Bennet continue in this same voluble vein all the while she is shown to her daughter's sick chamber ...

... And now she comes down, and she is still carrying on in exactly the same fashion as if she never stopped talking even while she was visiting her sick daughter. And I feel not a little sorry for Miss Bennet, whose aching head must have throbbed even more, having to listen to her mother's ceaseless prattling, when she must have wished to be left in peace.

Daughters with such a mother must have a great deal to bear.

* * * * *

So, Mrs Bennet assesses her daughter's condition as yet unfit for removal, and Miss Bennet is to remain at Netherfield a little longer.

I have this canny feeling that Mrs Bennet was determined to have her eldest's stay at Netherfield prolonged by hook or by crook, but given the fact that the doctor also was adamant that Miss Bennet should not yet be removed, it cannot be said that it was done by Mrs Bennet's contrivance alone.

I am quite surprised that Mrs Bennet's attitude towards my master is bordering on inimical. I would have expected someone of her ilk would be fawning over any young man of my master's fortune and standing in society, but it is not so. I have the distinct impression that she has some grudge against my master. I wonder if she senses that my master recoils from her vulgarity?

Chapter 5

'Unlike your haughty master' – that comment Miss Elizabeth once made upon my master comes back to niggle my mind. Considering his dawning infatuation for Miss Elizabeth, I cannot quite believe my master could have been openly uncivil either to Miss Elizabeth or to her mother, but my master being my master, he might have said or done something to offend them. Really his attitude, if not to say his personality, leaves much to be desired.

Chapter 6

In which the jealous Miss Bingley becomes a dog in the manger

I have come to know that Miss Elizabeth is an uncommonly intelligent lady. I am told that among tonnish gentlemen, an intelligent lady is not quite *à la mode* – even considered to be someone to be avoided – and is often given a rather pejorative epithet of a 'Blue Stocking'. But I can see that this prevalent opinion upon that topic is apparently not shared by my master. He seems quite fascinated by Miss Elizabeth's quick wit and sharp observational powers, which she employs with enchanting playfulness.

My master and Miss Elizabeth often become engaged in debates, which is an activity often fondly practised by my master with his friends, despite the fact that he is normally not of the talkative cast.

Oftentimes Miss Elizabeth has the edge upon my master in those debates, and I almost wince, fearing that my master might become awfully put out to be bested by a female, as it has often come to my notice that gentlemen abhor being beaten by ladies in anything at the best of times. But to my infinite relief and surprise, being bested by Miss Elizabeth seems to have very little adverse effect upon my master's ego. Instead, each defeat seems to strengthen his fascination for Miss Elizabeth yet further. Her every word seems to pull at something deep in him and be engraved, so to speak, into his heart. Human psychology is sometimes a very puzzling thing indeed.

These discussions thus carried out are often exclusive of others, and Miss Bingley is not amused. Her sour face becomes yet sourer on those occasions, and she invests great efforts in her endeavour to draw my master's attention away from Miss Elizabeth to herself.

She ever so often barges into their debates, disregarding whether or not the point she tries to make is as far removed from the pertinent point of the ongoing discussion as the Arctic is from the Antarctic.

On some occasions, she will just declare it is time for music, go and open the pianoforte, and play a piece as loudly as she is able, banging away the keys so that any talking will be impossible.

And on other occasions, she will insist that it be time to play at cards and they should stop engaging in silly talk, and will not take no for an answer.

And once, she even resorted to crying "Mouse!", and jumping onto a stool, went so far as to lifting the hem of her gown to such a daring level as to reveal her ankles, which she clearly thought was dainty enough to divert my master's attention from Miss Elizabeth and the debate.

Of course, a male being a male, my master did look at the ankles, but whether or not he thought them dainty was totally another matter.

Thus, interfere she will in a very dog-in-the-manger fashion which will impress any dog, with thoroughly blinkered single-mindedness.

What I dread is what Miss Bingley's reaction will be when she realizes her efforts are not producing any favourable result. What drastic measures would she take then?

A desperate lady, I have a sneaking suspicion, can be quite the scariest thing in the world.

* * * * *

To me, it is as plain as the sun at noonday that my master is held in thrall by Miss Elizabeth. Which fact, though, is totally unobserved by anybody else but Miss Bingley, it seems, as my master is a master pretender, a disguiser extraordinaire, who constantly assumes his firm sang froid exterior, and I believe that even jealously observant Miss Bingley has no notion of just how deep really is his fascination.

However, judging from what he lets slip to me in his unguarded moments, my master is trying his hardest not to fall in love with Miss Elizabeth. He takes his position as the head of the Darcy clan very seriously, and a punctilious individual rather lacking adaptability that he is, he has this awfully fixed notion that he must marry well.

Miss Elizabeth's station in society is far below my master's. Mr Bennet is a mere country gentleman with a smallish estate, and his wife is of far more modest lineage, and as you know, is, regrettably, awfully vulgar.

So, my master stubbornly adheres to the idea that as a Darcy, he should not be carried away by his passing fancy, and with groaning endeavour he forbids himself to fall deeper in Miss Elizabeth's thrall.

But it is my humble opinion that my master is fighting a losing battle. One's heart can never be bidden not to fall in love just as it can never be made to fall in love at one's bidding.

* * * * *

I am very curious what kind of conversation is exchanged in Miss Bennet's bedchamber between the two sister's, and unable to suppress my curiosity, I take this most welcome opportunity to slip into the room as Miss Elizabeth happens to open the door, and sit quietly in the corner to eavesdrop their conversation.

“Jane, I was really glad you were recovered enough to join the others in the drawing room this evening, albeit for only a couple of hours,” says Miss Elizabeth. “And so was Mr Bingley, which was written all over his face. He was solicitousness itself. It was obvious that in his eyes absolutely no one else existed when you were there in the room! Oh, Jane, I am sure he loves you dearly!”

Chapter 6

"Lizzy, you should not tease me so!" says Miss Bennet, blushing ever so becomingly.

"But, you do like him very much, Jane?" says Miss Elizabeth, looking into her sister's flushed face lovingly but with a mischievous smile.

"Of course, who indeed could help liking him?" answers Miss Bennet. "You like him, too, I think, Lizzy, do you not?"

"Oh, of course I do, but I dare say, you know very well my 'like' is an altogether different kind of like from yours."

"Oh, Lizzy, stop it!" says Miss Bennet, pressing the back of her palms against her hot cheeks as if to cool them. "Yes, because it is to you, I will speak honestly. I like him very much and I was happy he was so caring and so mindful of my comfort down in the drawing room. But Lizzy, I forbid myself to read too much into Mr Bingley's kindness, and am trying hard not to allow myself to think he really cares for me. Because the prospect is so heavenly that I am afraid of expecting too much only to find myself mistaken and suffer the consequence afterwards. Love turns one into a wretched coward."

"Oh, but I am sure you need not be afraid, as anyone who has eyes can see Mr Bingley is head over heels in love with you."

So, happy Mr Bingley. His love seems to be fully reciprocated. I hope my master's love will be, too ...

* * * * *

Today is Saturday, and it is four days since Miss Bennet became ill. Yesterday evening, as you would have gathered from the two sisters' conversation I related above, she was recovered enough to come down from her bedchamber and spend some time with the others. Mr Bingley's blooming face showed what happiness he derived from Miss Bennet's presence.

But this morning, the said gentleman's face is more downcast, as Miss Bennet has just declared that she has discommoded them long enough and it is time that she and her sister took their leave of Netherfield. Mr Bingley's earnest pleading, however, has earned another day's grace and she has agreed to accept their hospitality till tomorrow.

So, tomorrow the Misses Bennets are to leave.

I steal a secret glance at my master's face. The expression it bears is a complicated one. It is that of sorrow, but at the same time it is that of profound relief.

* * * * *

I overhear a conversation between Miss Bingley and Mrs Hurst as I happen to pass by the door of the Morning Room.

"What a great relief it is they are to leave Netherfield tomorrow!" cries Miss Bingley. "They certainly have grossly overstayed their welcome. If they had had any decency, they should have left days ago. Do you not agree, Louisa!?" Mrs Hurst here grunts assents. "And besides," Miss Bingley continues tirelessly, "Miss Eliza is so very irksome, and Mr Darcy indulges her far too much. It is so very vexing! She is one of of those contemptible females whose primary occupation in life is plotting and planning to draw gentlemen's attention. She is forever engaged in studying gentlemen's characters in order to discover what the best policies are to attract them and to act upon those findings accordingly. She must have decided that Mr Darcy finds pleasure in debating, and so she pretends she also has a predilection for discussions, and endeavours to monopolise his time as if no one else mattered. I wonder at Mr Darcy's being taken in so easily by such a paltry art! Is it not obvious that if Miss Eliza had found Mr Darcy fond of dancing, she would have been most eager to spend all the evenings dancing instead?"

"Precisely so," Mrs Hurst agrees with all alacrity. "We should take care, Caroline, so that Miss Eliza will not have any opportunity to be alone with Mr Darcy. Depend upon it. She is meaning to have him, and desperate to entrap him. God only knows what scheme she will try to contrive on this last day, if we are not vigilant. It is our sacred duty as the sisters of his closest friend to save him from whatever despicable scheme Miss Eliza might be plotting."

Chapter 6

The only likely person who is desperate enough to hatch such a scheme, I would have thought, is Miss Bingley.

* * * * *

Now, my master and Miss Elizabeth are in the family drawing room reading. Miss Bingley and Mrs Hurst, too – looking the very image of Gorgon sisters, whose fearsome visages are supposed to have turned those who saw them to stone – are seated in the same room, apparently determined to thwart Miss Elizabeth's 'despicable scheme' to be alone with my master.

By Mr Bingley's express wish, Miss Bennet has gone out to take a stroll in the grounds of Netherfield with that gentleman, as she had no opportunity to do so while she was confined in her bedchamber.

Contrary to Mr Bingley's sisters' accusations, I have not detected, in Miss Elizabeth's demeanour to my master, any indication that she may be wishing to secure my master's partiality. If anything, it is more like the reverse. I have seen something of defiance in her stance towards my master. Her eyes meet my master's with direct, challenging gaze. Of course, it could be argued that Miss Elizabeth might be a highly adept disguiser of feelings of my master's ilk, but I somehow doubt it.

My master, on this last day of the Misses Bennets' stay, seems to be making a determined effort to avoid contact with Miss Elizabeth, presumably owing to some notion he has formed – something silly like 'he has given too much attention to the lady already' or 'he had better curb his mounting fascination for her'. Such notions, in my opinion, are indeed exceedingly silly.

I have this hunch that Miss Elizabeth is the destined one for my master despite her low connections, which my master's connections are, in my opinion, plenty high enough to render unimportant. Their characters are very different, almost as different as 'darkness' and 'light', but the differences, I feel, are just such as would compliment each other's shortcomings and help form a perfect harmony. I do not know whether this is one of those intuitive feelings which animals are often said to possess or it merely comes from my wish that Miss Bingley will not prevail. Should it ever come to pass that Miss Bingley becomes my mistress, I would rather abscond by night, or if I use the vulgar parlance, 'shoot the moon'!

I wish to induce the two Gorgons to leave the room. A highly practical dog that I am, I should be able to devise something.

Oh! I have just accidentally nudged Mrs Hurst at the elbow, who has just been reaching for the vase to re-arrange the flowers, and have made her topple the vase over, which has caused the water to cascade down the front of both her and Miss Bingley's gowns!

They spring up from their seats, and begin to shake and pat the front of their gowns, and, most understandably, scream like banshees. They are just about to declare, I expect, that I am the most wretched and horrid of animals, when my master apologises on my behalf. Faced with my master's genial apology, they seem to lose their nerves to scold me, and are now turned all fawning smiles.

I will them to leave. They seem to hesitate for a moment, but the horror of showing my master their bedraggled forms seems to outweigh the dread of leaving my master and Miss Elizabeth alone, and to my great joy, they announce their intention to retire to their own chambers to change their apparel. Their hair is all messed up as well from the distressing event and the fuss they have made, and I know it will take at least full half hour for them to see to it that everything is put to rights, which will give my master a perfect opportunity to coze with Miss Elizabeth alone.

I am conscious of a wide grin spreading on my face, but am sure that my triumphant broad grin is not really discernible as such by the humans. They will assume I am only panting with my tongue out in my usual manner of breathing.

Am I a genius? I did not mean to cause the vase to topple over, and yet, without even trying, have succeeded so well. I must have been born with the genuine knack of getting in Miss Bingley's way.

So, my master is now left alone with Miss Elizabeth in the drawing room. I am itching with the urge to go and shut the door to give them cosy privacy. Though he is the stiffest and the most punctilious of sticklers for proper code of conduct, my master is, as I might have mentioned before, rather slow at those things, and I know perfectly well that he will not notice the impropriety even if I close the door. But I have not a clue what Miss Elizabeth's reaction will be, and do not wish to offend her sensitivity. My master will certainly not thank me for it, if I displease her. So I stay put grudgingly.

For all my effort, for all my fretting thus, though, my master most obdurately refuses to budge from his resolve not to converse with Miss Elizabeth, and will not give himself that indulgence and pleasure.

So, all my genius after all has been employed for nought. What a contrary, tiresome creature my master truly is!

* * * * *

It is Sunday. Misses Bennets are now gone from Netherfield, and it seems that my master is missing Miss Elizabeth's presence painfully.

If he feels so bereft now, methinks, he should have taken more care while Miss Elizabeth was here and should have made a little more endeavour to secure her regard, instead of hanging onto the silly notion that he should not let himself be carried away by a passing fancy.

Chapter 6

Chapter 7

In which my master's arch-enemy re-emerges

My master is greatly disturbed to have happened across Mr Wickham, his *bête-noire*, talking to the Bennet sisters in the street of Meryton this morning.

"Oh, Julius Caesar, old boy," my master cries, "who would have predicted Wickham, that infernal villain would re-emerge to intrude upon my path!? Wickham, attaining a commission and joining the very regiment stationed in Meryton! In Meryton of all places! And to cap all that iniquity, consorting with the Bennet sisters! Bennet sisters of all people!"

Mr Wickham, as you might remember, is the villainous gentleman who nearly despoiled Miss Darcy, my master's beloved sister, of her innocence once.

There is a long history in the connection between my master and this Mr Wickham. Mr Wickham is the son of my master's late father's steward, also deceased. Unlike his father, who was a brilliant steward and a highly esteemed, excellent man, Mr Wickham is a good-for-nothing. No, to dismiss him merely as a good-for-nothing would not quite explain the situation. To compare him to good-for-nothings would be an insult to the multitude of good-for-nothings, whose only crime is their good-for-nothingness. Mr Wickham is infinitely worse. His evil lies in his godless debauchery, his wanton extravagance, his lack of self-recrimination and his ruthlessness in gaining his own end, in doing which he does not care a whit whom he will trample over. He also loves gambling. If he were good at it, it would be something, but the trouble is that he is utterly useless at it and keeps on getting into debt. My master has often been applied to for help, which he has occasionally conferred. Not knowing Mr Wickham's real character, my master's father is said to have been fond of this wastrel son of his esteemed steward, and he entrusted his dying wish with my master that Mr Wickham be given the family living if he were to take holy orders in the future. But of course, as it was to be wholly predicted, Mr Wickham was never priest material. He asked my master for a pecuniary advancement in exchange for all the claim for the family living, making some plausible excuse that he wished to study law instead. My master complied and gave him three thousand pounds. A vast sum. But of course, he had no intention whatsoever of pursuing the law profession. He frittered away the three thousand pounds in a few years, at the end of which he had the nerve to apply to my master for more money. But this time, my master firmly refused to give any aid. Thus, forgetting it was all his own fault, Mr Wickham bore a grudge against my master, and the result was that he tried to elope with Miss Darcy, my master's beloved sister. Someone who could cold-heartedly scheme to injure such an angelic person as Miss Darcy can only be described as evil.

My master is especially worried because the worst thing about Mr Wickham is that his inner ugliness is not at all translated into his exterior. In fact he is an exceptionally handsome man with an appearance of uncommon decency and gentlemanliness. Indeed, if he looked even one tenth of the evil man that he really is, the situation would not be half as bad, if you understand my meaning.

My master frets over the possibility that Mr Wickham might bring his notorious charm to bear upon the Bennet sisters, and by saying

'Bennet sisters', I know he in truth means Miss Elizabeth. Of course, even very intelligent ladies are not immune to rakehells' charms, and the same may go for Miss Elizabeth. My master knows and I know that, though Mr Wickham will not have real interest in any lady without a hefty dowry, he will not have even a moment of hesitation before treading a path of wanton dalliance with any female who is at all willing. But my master has no cause for worry, as I am sure that Miss Elizabeth has far more sense than to allow any gentleman, let alone Mr Wickham, to take liberties upon her person, however attractive she might find him.

* * * * *

I have made friends with Dixon, an Irish Setter belonging to the kennel of Sir William Lucas of Lucas Lodge. I say 'belonging to Sir William's kennel', but Dixon informs me that he actually spends majority of his time with Miss Lucas when at home. Though he might not be the brightest of dogs, he is sufficiently intelligent and seems to understand what humans are talking about remarkably well.

According to Dixon, Miss Lucas is Miss Elizabeth's closest friend, and he often sits by Miss Lucas's side and listens to their conversation when Miss Elizabeth comes to visit her.

“My dear Julius Caesar,” says Dixon, “Miss Lucas is a very observant, frightfully perspicacious person. She thinks that your master, the august Mr Darcy, is quite smitten by Miss Elizabeth. What is your view upon it? Have you, too, that impression? You have said before, have you not, that your master imparts to you many things which he would not do to any humans? Has he ever confided in you concerning his feelings towards Miss Elizabeth?”

There is no harm in telling Dixon, methinks. After all, even if Dixon were to turn out to be a common gossip-monger and were to spread the rumour among other canines, there would be no danger whatsoever of any humans' finding it out.

“I, too, have that suspicion,” I say to him. “Although my master has never said it in any concrete words, I am sure that my master is greatly attracted to the lady."

"I hate to tell you this, Julius Caesar, but I shall have to give you a rather depressing piece of information concerning the subject," says Dixon. "Miss Elizabeth might not have a very good opinion of your master, which all seems to derive from your master's careless comment upon the lady at their first encounter. At the Meryton assembly, your master seems to have said something to the effect that Miss Elizabeth was not handsome enough to tempt him to dance with her. That comment, it appears, she most unfortunately overheard. Though I hear that she seemed to have been rather diverted than angered by the whole thing, and told all about it to Miss Lucas and others afterwards with great relish, she must have been not a little offended by the comment notwithstanding. What lady would not?"

Oh, God, no! That would never have done! How very thoughtless it was of my master! That is why I always worry about his abrupt ways!

"One's own words," Dixon muses, "may at any time come back to haunt one, so one should always be very very careful."

Dixon, as I said before, may not be the cleverest of dogs, but one cannot fault him in this most profound observation.

* * * * *

There is to be a grand ball here at Netherfield upon the twenty-sixth of November.

As the invitations have naturally been issued to all the officers of the regiment in Meryton, my master has been anticipating the inevitable meeting with Mr Wickham with the gravest disfavour, but as it has transpired, the said gentleman has declined the invitation making some excuses. No doubt, he has not the courage to appear in front of my master.

So, thus freed from the insalubrious prospect of having to come face to face with the detested man in front of the ballroom throng, my master is now able to concentrate his mind upon more pleasant prospects, and is looking forward with great pleasure to a chance to lead Miss Elizabeth to the dance floor for the first time.

I dearly hope that Miss Elizabeth will put aside the past injury, and look upon my master with more favourable eyes.

* * * * *

It is the night of the Netherfield Ball. Sir Lucas has kindly brought Dixon with him so that he and I can keep each other company in my quarter while our masters and mistresses are enjoying the night's entertainment.

"Has there been any advancement in the relationship between your master and Miss Elizabeth Bennet?" asks Dixon.

"Not that I know of," say I. "My master has been deuced looking forward to dancing with her, though, at today's ball."

"So, you think your master will ask her to dance? Miss Lucas certainly thinks so. She said to Miss Elizabeth that she was sure Mr Darcy would, then Miss Elizabeth said, 'Ah, but such an arrogant man as Mr Darcy, so very high in the instep, would never degrade himself by asking a mere country gentleman's daughter to dance with him at a ball. After all, I was not handsome enough to tempt him!' She said so rather jocularly. That remark, though, I thought, savoured some sort of grudge against the gentleman which she must still harbour in her heart. Do you not agree?"

And here again, I cannot fault him in his observation.

My master, if he were to wish to win Miss Elizabeth's affection, might have an uphill task. I really worry about him. I hope he will not dig an even deeper, bigger hole for himself tonight at the ball.

"By the by, have you ever met the officer called Wickham?" Dixon suddenly queries.

"Wickham!? Why do you ask?"

"Well, Miss Elizabeth seems to have been rather taken by him."

"Oh, no!" I cannot help letting out a loud cry.

"What is that loud 'Oh, no' for?" he asks. "What is wrong with the gentleman?"

Chapter 7

"Oh, everything is wrong with the gentleman!" I answer. "He is the lowest of the low, the worst of libertines! No one in petticoat is safe with that villain! A deflowerer of innocents, debaucher, profligate, gamester, cheat, spendthrift, you name any scoundrel, and he is one!"

"Is he that bad?"

I nod vigorously many times, and tell him all about his past sins.

"How many times my master gave him leases of life, you could not imagine! But my master was obliged to give him a firm 'No' in the end when things got far far too much. Then, would you believe it? Instead of castigating himself as was his due, he bore a deep grudge against my master, and even planned and plotted to insinuate his snaky way into my master's beloved sister's graces and elope with her! Of course, that was partly in order to get his dirty hands on her fortune, too! Is it any wonder that my master wishes that he would never have to set his eyes upon that villain ever again?"

"It is a pity, is it not, that we have no communicational means to warn the humans against Mr Wickham's evil ways?" says he.

"I wish my master would warn them, but he is very stubborn and thinks that becoming a tell-tale is far below his dignity. And in any event, this sort of thing is never that straightforward and needs to be handled with much care. And even if my master were to tell them about it, it would not necessarily follow that they would believe him. I just hope that Miss Elizabeth will be safe."

"She is my mistress's cherished friend and a deuced fine lady. And a cracking sport! I would hate it if any harm were to come to her. I will do what I can to deter Mr Wickham from having his way."

"Yes, I have not your kind of opportunity to be in her presence, so I shall depend on you. And moreover, I suddenly have this odd, most disturbing feeling, maybe a canine hunch, that I may not be here long to offer her help. Can I ask you a great favour, Dixon? Will you protect her to the best of your ability if I am not around?"

And Dixon solemnly gives me his word. He is a decent, dependable fellow, so I feel a little easier.

Chapter 7

* * * * *

My hunch was right. I shall not be here at Netherfield much longer. My master has resolved upon quitting Netherfield, possibly as early as tomorrow.

Despite having been up until very late after the ball last night, Mr Bingley rose early this morning and left for Town on some urgent business.

I have overheard my master's discourse with Mr Bingley's sisters.

It seems that, during the ball yesterday, it came to their notice that Mr Bingley's partiality towards Miss Bennet was of a far more serious kind than they had earlier thought. Mr Bingley, unlike my master, was always one who fell in and out of love very frequently. I do not mean he took love lightly. He would ever be a true gentleman and would never do anything which would compromise a lady. But it was a fact that, as Mr Bingley fell in love quickly, so did he fall out of love quickly, and it was natural that my master and Mr Bingley's two sisters assumed it was exactly the case with Miss Bennet as well. But as I said, during the ball yesterday, they suddenly realized that Mr Bingley loved Miss Bennet with wholly unprecedented seriousness and steadiness. And moreover, the notion suddenly rushed upon them that Mr Bingley's attachment had become a busily discussed topic in the neighbourhood. The realization made them decide that they should take some immediate measures to counteract such a rumour. To achieve that end, they have decided upon quitting Nethefield. They plan to advise Mr Bingley to remain in Town and stay away from Netherfield.

They deem the Bennets too low in social station to consider Miss Bennet as an eligible candidate for Mr Bingley. I grant that Mrs Bennet is staggeringly vulgar and two youngest Misses Bennets, a trifle fast, and I can see where their worries lie.

But it is my humble opinion that nothing good ever comes from meddling in other people's love affairs. I have once come across a saying from some exotic land of the Orient – it goes something like this: 'He who interferes with others' love should be kicked by a horse straight to hell'. Which I think carries much wisdom and edification, and one should take note of it.

Chapter 7

Chapter 8

In which, I accompany my master to London.

We have just arrived in London. Before leaving Netherfield, I heartily wished to have a final talk with Dixon, but I did not have that opportunity. I even ran to Lucas Lodge in the hope of meeting him, but he seemed to have gone somewhere with Miss Lucas, and though I waited as long as possible, he did not return.

If I were a human, I could send a missive to him notifying our departure, but as I am not, it cannot be helped. I trust that Dixon will understand my difficulty and forgive my discourtesy. I hope, true to his word, he will confer as much help as is possible in his power to Miss Elizabeth concerning the business of Mr Wickham. Of which help she will, I have no doubt, need plenty.

We have just arrived at Mr Darcy's London residence. Miss Darcy welcomes her brother and his guests very shyly as usual with her cheeks flushed with embarrassment, but with genuine good humour all the same.

Miss Darcy's new companion, a Mrs Annesley, a most genteel, genial looking lady in her middle age, with whom I have not had the honour of acquaintance so far, is standing beside her charge in an unobtrusive but protective and encouraging manner most pleasing to the eye. This lady's predecessor, Mrs Younge, was a viper in our midst, who abused her position as Miss Darcy's companion and lent her hand to Mr Wickham in his nefarious attempt upon Miss Darcy's innocence.

Taking that dreadful incident to heart, my master has taken especial care in choosing his sister's next companion, and I can see at a glance that the unstinting care my master has taken has born fruit most successfully.

* * * * *

Mr Bingley has been persuaded to remain in Town at least for the foreseeable future.

My master has convinced Mr Bingley that Miss Bennet's sentiment towards him is not what he hopes it is, and as such, the alliance between him and Miss Bennet is most inadvisable. You might wonder how my master could have achieved his objective so easily, but if you knew how the two gentlemen regard each other as well as I do, you would be able to guess easily. Mr Bingley places the highest reliance in my masters judgement and wisdom, and as it happens, whatever my master says is the law to Mr Bingley. To err is human; to forgive divine. But, in Mr Bingley's eyes, my master never errs – though in mine, he does, oftener than you might think ... Of course, some might say that five years' difference in their ages may sanction my master unquestioned supremacy, but in my opinion, blind reliance is, more often than not, a very dangerous thing.

Mr Binglely is to be a guest here in my master's London residence all the while he remains in London, instead of removing to his brother-in-law's in Grosvenor Street as he usually does.

* * * * *

It seems that we are to spend the whole of the festive season here in London this year. My master had previously settled upon spending it at Netherfield, and I suppose it is a little too late in the season to journey north all the way to Pemberley and then make preparations for the festivity there. I must admit that I usually much prefer spending Christmastide at Pemberley surrounded by all my friends in the kennel to spending it in Town. But of course, I am a humble canine companion, and my preference is of no consequence.

Mr Bingley seems awfully downcast. He must be missing Miss Bennet terribly. In fact my master seems so too, by which I mean 'missing Miss Elizabeth terribly'.

I suppose it is a good thing that Mr Bingley is thus dejected, as my master, instead of burying himself in gloom himself, puts his own sorrow aside and tries to do his very utmost to raise Mr Bingley's spirits, busying himself making plans for the festive season.

Busying oneself, I should imagine, is the best way to forget one's woes.

* * * * *

Now, Colonel Fitzwilliam, my master's cousin on the distaff side, older than him by two years, has come to visit my master to spend Christmas with him. My master's mother was a daughter of an earl, and her elder brother, the current earl, is Colonel Fitzwilliam's father.

Colonel Fitzwilliam is a gentlemanly, gentle gentleman, and I am vastly fond of him. Maybe because of the fact that they are similar in age, though in the ways of character, quite different, my master and Colonel Fitzwilliam are very close and love each other as if they were very best of brothers, and my master places considerable trust and reliance upon the Colonel, and vice versa.

They share what they call 'the ultimate ordeal' between them every year, that is, come the spring at Easter, they pay their duty to their formidable aunt, Lady Catherine de Bourgh of Rosings Park in Kent, together.

“What we would never be able to bear alone, we can just about tolerate if it is shared between us. An ordeal shared is an ordeal halved,” so they say. But then, they add, with a tone of utmost sincerity, “But, oh, how we wish we had a dozen more cousins to divide the burden of the ordeal yet further!”

* * * * *

As Miss Darcy was invited to dine with Mrs Hurst and Miss Bingley today, my master escorted her to Grosvenor Street, from where he has just returned.

Hardly has he come into his room when he calls out to me.

“Julius Caesar, my boy! I was shocked to find that Miss Bennet had called on Bingley's sisters at Grosvenor Street this morning! She seems to have come up to Town from Hertfordshire and been at her uncle's place for about a week. That was indeed a narrow escape. How fortunate it had been that I had insisted Bingley stay with me during his London sojourn instead of going to his brother-in-law's! He has barely recovered from the trauma of being separated from Miss Bennet. Had he been there and seen her, all the efforts we have made so far to make Bingley forget Miss Bennet would have come to nothing! Miss Bennet, according to Bingley's sisters, is going to be in London for a few months. I ought to remove Bingley to Derbyshire as soon as possible! But in the meantime, I have to keep him away from any public places Miss Bennet might visit!”

Chapter 8

Chapter 9

In which we travel to Pemberley, and I find that my master cherishes a miniature of a certain lady

We have arrived at Pemberley after six days of travelling. The journeys north hither have been very difficult, what with falling snow and mist, to say nothing of the precariousness of the frosty coating of the road-surfaces which concealed hazardous black ice underneath.

Mrs Hurst and Miss Bingley have been at their most irascible and abrasive, and everybody, Mr Bingley, Mr Hurst, their ladies' maids, the gentlemen's valets, and me, have all been at the receiving end of their continual vitriolic humour, but needless to say, with the sole exception of my master, to whom they have remained ever so pleasant.

* * * * *

Days are passing peacefully without many notable incidents here at Pemberley.

A couple days ago, I saw my master gazing at something in his hand, his facial expression one of contentment and tender sorrowfulness, a very faint poignant smile forming a very slight curve of his mouth. He, then, slid the object with especial care into the breast pocket of his coat next to his heart, and patted over it once or twice very softly as if to ensure it was there. I wondered then what it was to make him smile in that quietly satisfied, and yet at the same time touchingly pensive fashion afore mentioned.

Now, I have just caught him taking something out of the same pocket of his coat. I cannot suppress my curiosity and find it impossible to rest until I discover what it is. So, I assume a most casual air, saunter around the chair in which my master is seated, and stand unobtrusively behind my master where I should be able to command a good view of what my master has in his hand. It seems like a miniature of some sort. Without even stepping up closer, I think I know whose miniature it will prove to be. It must be Miss Elizabeth's. Who else could make my master smile and sigh in such a fashion? And now, I see, with a little closer inspection, it indeed is a miniature of the lady.

Noticing that I am looking, my master might even have blushed, were I a human, but as I am not, he has no cause for concern, or for feeling self-conscious. Instead, he seems not at all averse to talking about it. It is always a pleasurable thing, I have often been told, to speak of the one whom one is in love with.

Showing it to me proudly, “This, dear Julius Caesar, is a miniature of Miss Elizabeth,” says my master, rather superfluously, as I can see it perfectly without being told. “You may be wondering how I came by it,” continues my master. “In fact, I had secretly invited a skilful artist of my acquaintance to the Netherfield Ball expressly for the purpose of having him take her likeness. Of course, I had him take great pains to pretend that he was taking the likenesses of many other people, too, so as not to draw undue attention to the fact that it was Miss Elizabeth and Miss Elizabeth alone whom he was interested in. He seems to be endowed with some especial ability to memorize a person's face, as if it were imprinted in his brain. He says he can paint, if necessary, from memory without any long sitting sessions, once he has had a good and long look at a face. I had always known he was a very good artist, but Julius Caesar, do you not think this is remarkably fine? He has captured the lucent brilliance of Miss Elizabeth's eyes, the rather sassy curve of her rosebud mouth, and the translucent clearness of her skin touched slightly by the pink of a rose just so!"

I have seldom heard my master talk with so much expression in his voice before, as his usual mode of speech is not very much more than a drawling monotone.

'The lucent brilliance of the eyes', 'the sassy curve of the rosebud mouth', 'the translucent clearness of the skin touched slightly by the pink of a rose' indeed! My God! It is a perfect case of 'At the touch of love, everyone becomes a poet', as someone once cleverly put it.

"I have hit upon a capital idea," says my master, looking keenly at me. I have a very bad premonition. "As he is so fine an artist," my master continues, "why not have him take your likeness, too? I shall immediately send a missive to him and ask him to visit Pemberley."

Damn and blast! I am an active dog, a gun dog, well known for my highly athletic exploits! I am not one of those sedentary lap dogs, happy to be lazing about, perched upon a lady's lap. I think nothing of rushing around in the wild for hours on end, but sitting still in the same position for any length of time will drive me crazy.

But my father before me had also to sit for having his portrait painted next to his master, the late Mr Darcy, my master's father. So I shall have to take it as my lot and bear the torture, I suppose.

* * * * *

My master again takes out the miniature, and seems to find great delight in talking about Miss Elizabeth to me. He will never mention her name to anybody else, even to Mr Bingley, though I have just once heard him refer to Miss Elizabeth to Miss Darcy as a lady whom he is sure Miss Darcy would be very happy to be acquainted with. So, by and large I am the sole channel of release for his pent up emotion.

Chapter 9

Miss Bingley, who we thought was safely tucked away with her sister, her brother and her brother-in-law in the drawing room, suddenly sweeps into the library. My master calmly raises the hand holding the miniature to return it to his breast pocket. Miss Bingley's keen eyes seem to follow the movement of his fingers deuced closely until the very moment they let the miniature slide into the pocket.

"What was that you have just put into your pocket, Mr Darcy?" Miss Bingley, to my great surprise, has the audacity to ask such an impertinent question of my master.

"Nothing of any consequence which might concern Miss Bingley," answers my master with cold poise.

Did she hear my master mention Miss Elizabeth's name? Did she guess what it was that my master put back to his pocket? I do not know. But she bites her lower lip as if she did.

* * * * *

I now sit still, having my likeness taken. As I thought, sitting thus for a long time is tedium itself, and I am sure it will give me a deuced stiff neck later. I do not know how others can bear it. Of course, I can at any time stand up and walk if I so choose, pretending not to be at all aware that it is to be frowned upon for a model even to fidget. I am a mere canine companion after all, and no one would really expect me to understand the solemnity of the occasion. But it is a matter of pride. I have to show that I am no ordinary dog, but a pattern of excellence.

My master has his miniature again in his hand, and is discoursing with the artist about the excellence of his execution, the fineness of his brush strokes, and the purity of his colours. The artist is the only human to whom my master mentions anything of the miniature and the lady therein, and he takes great delight in the opportunity to do so.

Some comment induces my master to rise, and to go and stand beside the artist to show the miniature to him, who takes it in his hand.

Here, an unexpected misfortune occurs.

Chapter 9

Miss Bingley again suddenly barges in without even a by-your-leave, and surprises the artist, causing him to let the miniature slip through his fingers to the floor. The floor is covered with a thick and luxurious carpet, so there is, thanks be to God, little danger of the fall doing any damage to the miniature. But the worse danger looms elsewhere. The miniature rolls towards Miss Bingley, instead of away from her. She, I am persuaded, has seen it is a miniature, but she is not near enough to see of whom. Her eyes glisten with anticipation and she edges towards where the miniature is.

Damnation! She will see it!

I, cleanly forgetting my role as the sitting model, take upon myself the charge of the situation, and with the speed of lightning, run towards the miniature and before Miss Bingley has time to bend over it, cover it with my paws. Thinking it may not be sufficient, I next shift my whole body over it and await my master's administration.

Miss Bingley, exceedingly curious and unutterably piqued, no doubt wishes to push me, or rather, kick me to the side to get to what is under my abdomen. But she is clearly in a sad quandary. However desperately she might wish to get her hand upon the miniature, she cannot manhandle me or behave in any indecorous manner in front of my master.

My master slowly comes to my side, pats my head and back, and fishes out the miniature from under me, which tickles me a little, and slides it into his pocket with rather deliberate calmness in front of Miss Bingley's very nose to her absolute chagrin.

* * * * *

Coming to the sudden realization that the most effective method to guard my master against Miss Bingley's machinations is not to stay by my master's side all the time as I have so far been doing, but to keep a constant eye upon Miss Bingley herself, I now follow Miss Bingley closely, sometimes overtly, but mostly in covert operation.

Since that episode concerning the miniature that I mentioned above,

Miss Bingley has been making persistent efforts to discover whose likeness is depicted in the miniature which Mr Darcy keeps in so cherishing a manner next to his heart. She has been trying all sorts of tricks.

She has tried to draw information with oblique questions from Mr Meadows, the butler, and Mrs Reynolds, the housekeeper, in which she has failed. She has used more direst queries with the parlour maids and the first, the second, and the third footmen, in which attempts, either, she has not been successful. She seems to have even tried bribery with the chambermaids and lower footmen. But it has produced no wished for outcome. It has only proved that none of them knows anything of the miniature in question.

Thus, concluding that the last resort will be my master's valet, Mr Trent, she is now about to try her luck with him.

She waylays him.

"Ah, Trent," says she, passing by him, and looks over her shoulder, feigning to be just *en passant*, "I just remembered. I found a miniature in the drawing room after the guests had left, and I do not know whom it belongs to. But I seem to recall Mr Darcy, too, has a miniature of some lady. Am I not right?"

Mr Trent answers in the affirmative, not being aware that my master does not wish it known to Miss Bingley.

"I have been wondering if it is Mr Darcy's," continues Miss Bingley, fabricating a story. "Of course, it is more likely to belong to one of the guests as I seem to recall one of the gentlemen showing a miniature of his wife to my sister. But I just thought I should ask you first in case it is Mr Darcy's. It is ... a picture of a lady with ... dark hair and dark eyes."

"Yes, my master's miniature does bear a lady with dark hair and extraordinarily fine dark eyes," says Mr Trent.

"A few curls adorning the cheeks?"

"Yes, that is right. But if it is my master's, you would probably have recognized the lady in the miniature, because I trust it is one of the ladies with whom you are well acquainted, too," says Mr Trent to my consternation. Oh, no, do not divulge so much!

"A lady I am also acquainted with?" she stands alert. "What is her name?" Miss Bingley queries a little sharply. Oh, no, do not give her name away!

"That, I regret to say, I cannot remember," Mr Trent says, to my great relief. But then, I think to myself. Mr Trent not remembering Miss Elizabeth's name? Can it be possible? He is one of those people who never forget people's names.

"Where did I first have the honour of her acquaintance, or where did Mr Darcy, for that matter?" Miss Bingley persists. Oh, no! Please do not say Hertfordshire!

"Eh ... that, either, I cannot quite recall," says Mr Trent. "Was it here at Pemberley? London?" he continues, tilting his head to the side, tapping his chin lightly and frowning a little, as if thinking hard to remember. "No, Bath!" he corrects himself. Then, "Or ... could it have been Tunbridge Wells? But then again, it might have been Brighton, or even Edinburgh ..." Then, I realize that Mr Trent is indeed teasing Miss Bingley. And I heave a sigh of relief.

"How long has Mr Darcy had the miniature?" she asks next, clearly not realizing she is being teased.

"I cannot recall exactly how long, but I think for quite a few years," Mr Trent says rather mendaciously.

"For a few years?" muses Miss Bingley, and seems to be content that the miniature cannot be that of Miss Elizabeth. Then, Miss Bingley's face suddenly burgeons into a wide smile.

A deuced ill omen! I have a bad, bad feeling here. Oh, hells bells! She is thinking the miniature must be that of herself! After all, Miss Bingley, too, has dark hair, dark eyes (of course, hers could never be referred to as 'extraordinarily fine', but ladies, I have often noticed, have a great tendency to overestimate their own attributes), and curls around the cheeks!

"Oh, Trent, you jest!" she cries in sudden good spirits, "I might be slightly acquainted with the lady, too, indeed!" And she all but taps Mr

Trent's arm with her fan jocularly almost with coquetry.

And I groan, convinced that Miss Bingley does indeed believe it to be a miniature of her own self. Her self-conceit has reached a level which almost impresses me.

Mr Trent looks not a little taken aback by this extravagant show of joviality of hers, and staggers back a pace.

Has he any idea what he has just done? Giving Miss Bingley such a wrong notion is very dangerous. Oh, God! She will lavish her fawning attention upon my master even more!

* * * * *

Directly after that, Miss Bingley hurries to her sister's chamber, and I follow her.

"Louisa!" with tremendous energy, she flings open the door, which bounces back almost to her face, but totally unchecked by that, she cries, "Oh, you will never never guess! Oh, happy, happy, happy we!"

"Whatever is the matter with you, Caroline!? You sound like Galatea from Handael's opera! Calm yourself! Do not shout!" chides Mrs Hurst.

"Calm myself!? This is not the time for being calm! And how can I not shout! What do you think, Louisa!? Mr Darcy loves me!"

"Eh!?" Mrs Hurst lets out an incredulous cry, and asks with her eyes almost popping out. "Mr Darcy loves you!? Has he offered for you at last!?"

"No, silly! As if Mr Darcy would be so precipitous!" Miss Bingley chuckles. "But what do you think? Have a guess!"

"How can I have a guess with so little clue?"

"Oh, then, I will give you a clue! His miniature! There!"

"His miniature!? You mean, the miniature you told me you thought Mr Darcy kept in his breast pocket? You said, if I remember rightly, you did not know whose likeness it was, but suspected it was that of someone of our acquaintance? Someone not at all worthy of Mr Darcy, you said?"

"Yes, but I was utterly mistaken! And whose likeness do you think it is, Louisa!? The lady in question has now turned out to be me! Me!"

"What do you mean the lady in question has turned out to be you?"

"Exactly what I say. I am the lady on the miniature!"

Mrs Hurst seems to have lost her voice here. There is a momentary silence.

"Caroline, have you been dreaming?" Mrs Hurst after a while asks in a doubting tone.

"What do you mean Have I been dreaming?" Miss Bingley says, sounding not a little affronted. "Are you insinuating that I can't possibly be the model in the miniature?"

"But how can it possibly be you? You have never sat for it, Caroline."

"Oh, a man in love could achieve an awful lot, Louisa! Surely, even you know that is a fact. Mr Darcy must have had my likeness taken in strict secret. A man in love could sometimes be so secretive. And besides, he would have had plenty of opportunities as I have been in his company so very often! You must agree, Louisa."

"Well, if you insist. So, do I understand you have actually seen the miniature?"

"No, I have not seen the miniature *per se*," Miss Bingley says a little defensively, "but Trent all but said so. According to him, the lady in the miniature has dark hair and dark eyes, and curls around the cheeks."

"Caroline, you are by no means the only young lady with dark hair and eyes, and curls. Miss Eliza Bennet, for one ..."

"Of course, I am well aware of that!" interjects Miss Bingley rather petulantly. "But upon Trent's authority, and you will agree his authority must be the most reliable, Mr Darcy has had the miniature for a few years, so it cannot be that of Miss Eliza, can it? And he had that very meaningful look upon his face when he imparted that information to me, as if ... as if he wished me to understand the hidden significance for his master's sake. Oh, I am sure of it!"

"Mr Darcy never looks like a man deeply in love when he is with you, though, Caroline," says Mrs Hurst, apparently still not quite convinced.

"Oh, you know very well what Mr Darcy is like! He is so stoical, so reserved. He is the kind of man who will shudder at showing his feelings towards a lady unless he is absolutely secure of the lady's returning his love. He will not act until he has absolute conviction. I am afraid, Louisa, I have so far been much too reticent."

Miss Bingley, reticent!? I do not know how I have managed to prevent a loud snort breaking out of my nose. If there can be a man who does not notice so unsubtle and profuse expressions of love and so desperate a pursuit of himself, he can only be a total imbecile or a dead man.

Chapter 9

Chapter 10

In which the deluded Miss Bingley launches a string of attacks upon my master

I am painfully aware that Miss Bingley is driven and determined. She seems to believe that the only reason why my master has not had the courage to propose, is that he still feels too shy to do so. She is convinced that she should give him some encouragement or even some nudge, a forceful nudge to be precise, to make him take the final plunge. Nothing can be more scary than a deluded woman's logic.

Every day I am on edge. I have no one to turn to but myself. No one knows of her desperate scheming. I keep a constant vigil, and follow her everywhere like a shadow. But on no account must I let her know that I am doing so. Undoubtedly, at least at the present moment, she believes I am a mere dog and have no notion what occurs in the human world, but a desperate female could sometimes become incredibly sentient.

My master, on the other hand, has no notion whatsoever of Miss Bingley's conviction as regards his miniature, so he is bamboozled by her constant fluttering of eyelashes at him and her cooing familiarity with him.

Mr Trent, either having no idea of the impact his little teasing of Miss Bingley has produced or deliberately keeping mum suspecting the enormity of it, has obviously not confessed it to my master.

One good thing that has accrued from it, is that Miss Bingley thinks the lady in the miniature is Miss Elizabeth no more. But whether or not the fact that she believes herself to be the lady whose picture my master keeps so close to his heart, is a case of 'the lesser of the two evils', is as yet uncertain.

* * * * *

My master is much harassed and wearied by Miss Bingley's unceasing pursuit of him hither, yon and everywhere, but as it is impossible to be more blunt than he has already been without employing expressions of downright rudeness, he is at his wits' end what to say or do.

So, in a desperate bid to prevent her from following him, he has declared to everybody instead, presumably in the scant hope that she will take his meaning without being told in the rudest of terms, that he has much estate business to attend to and wishes to be excused to retire to the library for a while to pore over his ledgers unhindered and undisturbed by anybody, and is bidding them not follow him, telling them that the library shall remain strictly a room to which entrance is forbidden for the next few hours.

He is making a fatal mistake! I immediately sense what direction Miss Bingley's mind is taking. In her deluded mind, that kind of declaration from my master constitutes only one thing – an unassailably plain invitation for her, and her alone, to follow him.

How my master, undoubtedly a man of great intellect, has failed to anticipate that happening is beyond my comprehension.

My master leaves the room, without any notion what calamity he might just have begotten for himself, and Miss Bingley, the cunning lady that she is, will bide a while until she can make a plausible excuse and slip out of the room in hot pursuit of my master.

I need to think quickly and act swiftly.

Chapter 10

I run to Mr Trent. After all, all this is his fault, so he should be the one responsible for finding the remedy for the situation.

He, it seems, is beginning to realize that the blame for Miss Bingley's persistence should be laid at his door, and is feeling not a little guilty. So, when I seek help, or to be more precise, whenever I draw his attention to her when she is about to make an assault upon my master, he is willing to do anything to lessen the damage which his own careless teasing of Miss Bingley has wrought upon my master.

Thus, on this occasion, too, when I find him and tug him by the sleeve, denoting I wish him to follow me, he stands up and follows me without delay. I head the way, as Mr Trent would not know where my master is.

When we are upon the lower landing just before we reach the corridor leading up to the library, we look down, and see Miss Bingley walk past the foot of the staircase in the direction of the library. She looks back once or twice as if making sure no one is nearby, but she fails to look up the stairs to the landing where we are.

We swiftly walk down the stairs, taking care not to make noise so as not to alert Miss Bingley. Our footsteps are very quiet upon the thick stair carpet, so Miss Bingley will be unaware that we are hot on her heels. Reaching the foot of the stairs, Mr Trent and I peep round the corner, and see Miss Bingley, just arriving at the library door, turn the knob quietly, open the door, and walk in. We dash to the door, and before Miss Bingley has time to close it, Mr Trent is there to prevent it from shutting. I would not be at all surprised if she had even been planning to lock the door behind her.

Miss Bingley momentarily looks utterly exasperated to have been thus foiled in her scheme, but probably deciding that it would make Mr Trent suspicious of her if she stays angry, she at once recovers, and in a purposely cheerful, carefree voice, says,

"Oh, you gave me a scare, Trent!"

"I beg you pardon, Miss Bingley. I am looking for my master," says Mr Trent, casually craning his neck as if to make good what he tells her is the truth.

"Eh? Is Mr Darcy in here?" she queries as if she were surprised. "Oh Mr Darcy, you are here! Oh, yes, now come to think of it, you did say that you were coming to the library to pore over your ledgers and did not wish to be disturbed. I have completely forgotten!" says the mendacious lady. "Please forgive me. How mortified I shall feel if I have inadvertently disturbed you, Mr Darcy!"

Inadvertently, indeed! Nothing could have been more deliberate.

"Not at all. Please do not think anything of it, Miss Bingley," says my master politely enough, but in an uninterested monotone. "But as I said, I am a little busy, so please excuse me."

⁂ ⁂ ⁂ ⁂ ⁂

My master has become thoroughly fatigued by Miss Bingley's perpetually hovering around him, and seems to have concluded that on such a bleak mid-winter day, she would not chase him if he goes outside. And thus, he heads for the freezing summerhouse to take refuge.

But a lady who is bent on pursuing her prey will not be deterred by a mere threat of getting one chilblain or two, and Miss Bingley is showing every sign to be determined to follow him.

I do not wish to be thought a one-trick pony, but I cannot think of any other way impromptu. So, I run to Mr Trent yet again.

I find him, and lead him to the window from which the expanse of the grounds can be seen. At some distance to the north-west, we see the summerhouse, towards which a male figure, to wit, my master, is heading. I draw Mr Trent's attention to a female figure, to wit, Miss Bingley, which has just emerged from round the far corner of the east wing, and is obviously in hot pursuit of my master.

"You do not like Miss Bingley much, do you Julius Caesar?" says Mr Trent. "She is rather harsh to you when Master is not looking. It is quite natural for a dog to harbour a dislike towards an individual who is apparently not very kind to animals. So, you hate it when she goes near your master, is it not so? Your are jealously guarding your master. You are a good boy." And he pats my head.

Fortunately, Mr Trent, it seems, does not suspect the real extent of intelligence with which I am endowed, nor does he find the fact overly suspicious that I try to sabotage any scheme Miss Bingley gets up to. He appears to dismiss my interference as something a dog would normally do.

"And I suppose you now want me to prevent her from following Master, do you not?" he says. But I have a feeling that he is just using me as a pretext for what he is about to do. "Humm ..." he muses, tapping his chin with his forefinger, which I am beginning to learn is the gesture he always makes when he is forming a cunning plan.

As it happens, it had been snowing heavily for many days until a few days ago, and upon the roof is thickly laid snow. Fortunately, the sun has been shining and the hold of the snow is loosening, and a little push will guarantee the avalanche of the snow.

Miss Bingley, who is religiously following the circuitous path swept free of the snow, will in a short time pass by the eaves of the roof directly below our window.

Mr Trent looks around in search of, apparently, something to give the snow a necessary nudge with.

"This will do," he says, having found a sturdy looking broom, and gives the edge of the snow a mighty push just as Miss Bingley passes. We hear a lady's horrified scream from below an instant later, which confirms us that Mr Trent's scheme has worked to a tee.

I run down the stairs to see the result of Mr Trent's effort, and hurry to the nearest door to the spot. I almost collide into Miss Bingley, who is entering the house through the door, miserably bedraggled and upon the very verge of hysterical tears.

Mr Trent, too, is at my heels, and sees Miss Bingley.

"Good Lord, Miss Bingley! Whatever has happened to you!? Are you all right? You are drenched! I hope you are not injured!" he says in a tone of deceptively sincere solicitousness and astounding innocence.

"Oh, Trent! That wretched snow!" she wails. "How dared it fall upon me! Just as I was about to ... !"

And here she halts. She could hardly admit, "Just as I was about to chase after Mr Darcy."

"There, there, Miss Bingley," says Mr Trent, "You had better hurry to your room before you catch your death. I will immediately see to it that a hot bath be prepared for you."

Mr Trent is exactly a valet after my own heart, well deserving to serve my master.

Chapter 10

Chapter 11

In which Miss Bingley resorts to desperate measures

Having failed in all else, Miss Bingley is, I have good reason to believe, planning to begin an assault upon my master in the middle of the night. Exactly what form it will take, I have not yet had means of discovering, but I have not a speck of doubt that the measures she will pursue will be rather major than minor. So, I am all alertness at all times to be ready to frustrate her plans.

Now it is at least an hour past midnight.

My master is fast asleep. I creep out of his room, and hurry to Miss Bingley's chamber. When I approach her room, by dint of the light seen through the narrow fissure beneath the door, I see Miss Bingley's candles still burning. I walk past her door, and go and sit in the shadow of the shallow alcove located just a short way from the door, and wait.

About a quarter of an hour elapses, when the door slowly opens, and Miss Bingley pokes her head out and looks to the right then to the left surreptitiously several times. But of course she does not see me, being hidden tucked in the alcove. She then, as if satisfied that nobody is by, steps out into the corridor, and I see she has a small lamp in her hand. She begins gingerly to make her way along the corridor in the direction of my master's chamber. I hug the shadows and follow Miss Bingley as closely as I dare. Her progress is very slow as if she is not quite sure of her own intention. But it is probably because her lamp is most part covered so that it will not emit too much light, and she has to take care to be sure of her footing.

I have a strong suspicion that under her night gown, she has a flimsy night dress with dainty frills and such, which I am certain she believes would stir any young male's blood hotly running through his veins. I doubt very much, however, that it would stir my master's. It would be far more likely to freeze it instead. A lady with proper sense of decorum should not be skulking about the house at the dead of night in such attire anyways. My acute auditory sense detects the faint sound of her teeth chattering, presumably from cold, but it could well be from some sense of dread or uncertainty about the justness and rightness of whatever reckless act she is about to carry out.

I cannot think of any other solution. I ought to wake Mr Trent, who sleeps in the attendant's room adjacent to my master's, drag him out of bed by whatever means, bring him out into the corridor, and pre-empt Miss Bingley before she can reach my master's bedchamber.

How can I pass by Miss Bingley without her realizing I am here? Luckily for me, as I mentioned before, her lamp is for a most part covered and does not give out much light, only lighting up a couple of feet ahead of her at the most. My night vision is, naturally, far better than Miss Bingley's. Our ability to see in darkness must be at least five times superior to that of humans'. One has to acknowledge that felines are even better endowed therewith, but when one thinks of how much better canines are blessed in any other sphere, one should know how to be content.

So, if I can somehow successfully pass by Miss Bingley and gain a few yards' advantage without her seeing me, she will remain totally ignorant of my presence.

We are soon to come to the wide gallery at the top of the stairs, along whose wall facing the wide staircase under the massive portrait of my master's father with my father beside him is placed a very long table with some ornaments upon it. I think quickly and decide it is the only option. If I run under it swiftly while Miss Bingley slowly treads her way, I should be able to come out on the other side having gained a few yards easily while she manages to advance only a couple.

As soon as she comes level with the edge of the table, therefore, I commence running under it. It is quite a feat to do so at one's utmost speed while trying not to bump into its legs, especially when one's tail tends to swing from side to side when one runs and one has to remember to curb its movement to the minimum. When one thinks of the priceless vases and ornaments which are placed upon the table, in spite of the chilly air, one feels as if sweat were oozing out of one's foot pads. If I were a human, sweat would be forming upon my brows, but we dogs do not sweat as humans do. It is indeed a blessing. I would hate it if sweat were running down my brows into my eyes obscuring my vision. I momentarily feel worried that the sweat oozing out of my foot pads might make my paws slippery, but to my great relief, it seems to have no adverse effect.

There! I have managed to come out without even once as much as brushing the table's legs! As I continue to run forward, while glancing backwards to see where Miss Bingley is, I am fully satisfied to note she is lagging far behind. I run as fast as I am able, and come to the door to Mr Trent's room.

I open the door and rush in.

I hear Mr Trent's loud snoring. I feel terribly sorry to wake someone sleeping so soundly, but needs must when the devil drives.

I run up to the bed, jump onto it, sink my teeth into his bedding and tug it back, all the while stamping on Mr Trent's abdomen, hoping to wake him. He is a damned deep sleeper, but even a deep sleeper could not sleep through that commotion. He opens his eyes dazedly. There is no time to lose. I lock my jaw into his nightshirt sleeve next, and begin frantically to pull it. I think his immediate thought when his sleepy head clears enough to see who or what is disturbing him is that something might be amiss with my master, so he jumps up without delay and grabs hold of his coat, throws it over his shoulders, and follows me out into the corridor.

Mr Trent and I tumble out of the door just as Miss Bingley arrives at the door to my master's bedchamber and is about to place her hand upon the doorknob.

"Miss Bingley!" cries out Mr Trent, "What on earth are you doing here at this time of the night!?"

Miss Bingley freezes. I can almost hear her brain working rapidly.

She stands there completely motionless for a long while. I wait with bated breaths for her next move. Then she turns round little by little, like a lifeless doll on a very slow pivot, her face vacant, devoid of any expression, her eyes hollow, looking straight ahead like unseeing eyes gazing at a void. She, then, in an extremely slow movement, takes one step forward, and then another, as though she were someone sleepwalking ...

"Miss Bingley!" calls Mr Trent again, this time much louder.

Miss Bingley flinches visibly, and blinks hard many times, then, as if just woken up, vaguely looks about her.

"Oh! Where am I? What am I doing here?" she queries.

I am devilish impressed. What a brilliant actress she is! Had I not seen her emerge from her bedchamber so surreptitiously, cast her keen eye about hither and thither, clearly in possession of her whole faculty and looking anything but a sleepwalker, I would be completely taken in by her now, as Mr Trent seems to be. Or is he?

"Why, Miss Bingley! How extraordinary! Do you really not remember anything? You must have been sleepwalking!"

"I? Sleepwalking? Is it true? Oh, how mortifying!" says she, covering her cheeks with her hands, but no doubt, finding it much less mortifying to be thought a sleepwalker than to be known to have been planning to visit my master's bedchamber under cover of night.

"Oh, I would often sleepwalk as a small child," says she – I cannot quite tell whether it is a fact or a fabrication – "but I have not done so for a long time. Maybe I have eaten something difficult to digest. When I think about it now, I do, I dare say, feel something lying heavily upon my stomach. That was always the case when I was a child. A heavy stomach would either give me a nightmare or make me sleepwalk."

She is not only a highly convincing actress, but also a master story-teller, it seems.

"You had better return to your room, Miss Bingley," says Mr Trent, "before you catch your death (this is the second time Mr Trent has used the expression in as many days), and before my master wakes. You, I am sure, would not wish him to know that you have been roaming about the corridors in the night."

"Oh, no, indeed! I would have felt deeply embarrassed and humiliated if it had been Mr Darcy who caught me in such dishabille!" says Miss Bingley, as if exactly such, or something even far more daring, had not been her true aim.

"It was indeed fortunate that you did not come to any harm," adds Mr Trent. "You could easily have fallen to the floor and injured yourself, or even fallen down the stairs! How lucky it was for you that Julius Caesar was there to wake and alert me!" says Mr Trent. Oh, no! Now, Miss Bingley knows that it was I again that frustrated her carefully planned scheme! It is Mr Trent's decided tendency, it seems, to blurt out something which is much better to be left unsaid.

"Yes, indeed, how I owe it to Julius Caesar that I was saved from a possible injury and even mortification! How I wish to thank him for according me such opportune assistance!" cries Miss Bingley, almost gnashing her teeth, and then, eyes me in a most menacing fashion.

I have a feeling that Miss Bingley might be beginning to suspect strongly that there might be far more intelligence in me than meets the eye. It is, I should imagine, inevitable.

So now, Miss Bingley gone, all is quiet again outside my master's bedchamber. I open the door and go in. Faint snoring is heard from my master's bed, which tells me that my master has peacefully slept through that commotion. Thank god for that!

* * * * *

Tomorrow, we are all to leave Derbyshire for London. This evening, all are as usual gathered in the drawing room after dinner.

Mr Bingley has just challenged my master to a game of billiards. Even Mr Hurst, who is normally indolent beyond description, pronounces his willingness for a game or two to everybody's great surprise. The ladies voice their wish to be allowed to watch the game and insist they will not be gainsaid. So the ladies and the gentlemen all stand up to remove themselves to the Billiard Room.

In the Billiard Room, the gentlemen beg the ladies their forgiveness, and take off their coats to make themselves more comfortable and freely mobile for the sport.

First, my master and Mr Bingley take up their respective cues, and the battle commences. Their skills are fairly well matched. During a game of billiards is virtually the only occasion on which Mr Bingley becomes quite aggressive against his usual insouciant nature.

I always become awfully excited and deeply fascinated whenever I watch billiard games played, and my master always permits me to sit on one of the chairs so that I could view the game. He sometimes even allows me some especial indulgence to go on the billiard table and chase the balls when he practises alone. Oh, how I enjoy those occasions!

As usual, I become utterly absorbed in watching, and all else recedes and I only see the activity around the billiard table. The crisp sound of the billiard balls colliding, the manner in which the balls move sharply and hit the pockets, the way the gentlemen position their arms and cues, and the beautiful line of their postures when they pause just before they thrust the cue forward ...

But suddenly, it comes into my conscious mind that I have been for some time vaguely aware, in the periphery of my vision, of some movement somewhere around the raised arm of the chaise-longue over which my master formerly threw his coat carelessly.

Chapter 11

I turn round, and see Miss Darcy standing just behind me to the right, then Mrs Hurst stationed behind Miss Darcy a little to the left in front of the chaise-longue, and Miss Bingley, positioned in between Mrs Hurst and the chaise, effectively hidden from everybody's vision, acting in a most suspicious manner, ... seems to have her hands upon my master's coat!

But I seem to have noticed it too late as, whatever she may have been doing, she appears to have achieved the aim, and she now steps a pace forward, and stands next to Mrs Hurst. Whether or not Mrs Hurst has been party to what Miss Bingley has been doing, I do not know, but Mrs Hurst smiles at Miss Bingley, who does not at all seem inclined to return the smile.

Judging from her humour, there is very little doubt that Miss Bingley has achieved success in finding out the identity of the mystery lady in my master's miniature. Is she ruing her own folly in so zealously trying to discover the lady's identity, only to be bitterly disappointed?

In the end, it is probably for the best if Miss Bingley has indeed found that the miniature irrefutably bears the likeness of Miss Elizabeth's, not hers. At least, she will henceforward not deceive herself, and will discard that utterly silly notion that my master only needs encouragement to be brought to do her the honour of offering his hand in marriage.

May my master be left in peace! Maybe it is the divine Providence that we are to leave for London tomorrow, and from thence, my master and guests are to part their ways, if only for a few weeks. My master is going into Kent to visit his aunt, Lady Catherine de Bourgh, while the Bingleys and the Hursts are heading for Brighton, before they all meet again in Town, where they will remain till the end of the Season.

Chapter 11

Chapter 12

In which my master travels to London, then on to Kent, where he comes across the love of his life again

We left Derbyshire the day before yesterday and have just arrived in Town.

Miss Bingley's mood is a difficult one to define. As an army general must rearrange his strategy according to which direction the wind blows, so she seems to be reassessing the situation. One thing is certain, though. She will not abandon the offensive so easily.

Mr Bingley, Miss Bingley and the Hursts will leave tomorrow to return to Grosvenor Street, before setting out to Brighton, and peace will be restored to my master, at least for a while.

Colonel Fitzwilliam is expected to commence his furlough tomorrow and come to my master's residence without delay. He and my master will, then, travel to Kent.

* * * * *

The carriage carrying my master and Colonel Fitzwilliam is now trundling along the road to Kent at a leisurely pace. I am as usual allowed to travel with them in the carriage.

"Oh, what is this?" says Colonel Fitzwilliam, patting his coat pocket, noticing a rustling sound when touched, and fishes out something from there. "Oh, yes, Wickham's letter to you. I was going to give it back to you in London, but I completely forgot."

"Eh, which one was that?"

"The one acknowledging the receipt of the three thousand pounds from you, as the immediate pecuniary advancement in exchange for any future claim upon the living in your gift. Shall I give the letter back to you now, or shall I keep it till we go back to London?"

"It does not matter which way," says my master casually. "But just give it to me now. I will put it in my drawer in Rosings. By the by, did you manage to discover who those friends of his were, whom he mentioned in the letter?"

"Yes, as we thought, they are Mrs Younge's brothers. They used to be, or probably still are, Wickham's gambling cronies. Real hardened gamesters, I heard."

"So, they were the link between Wickham and Mrs Younge," says my master. "I wondered how those two got to know each other so well."

"Talking of Wickham and Mrs Younge, Georgiana, I am happy to note, has regained the cheerfulness of her former self before the ordeal of last summer. I hope she is not worrying her pretty head about Wickham any more."

"I think she was only persuaded into believing herself in love by that silver-tongued villain in the first place," answers my master. "She is a level-headed girl. Once she sat down and reflected upon her own true feelings away from his coercing influence, she soon realized that it was nothing but a delusion."

"It must have been a godly intervention that Georgiana was saved by your timely arrival. Had she eloped with that villain, living out her life in the mire of bitter regrets would without a doubt have been her lot. It often happens that a momentary infatuation takes over one's brain and makes one behave in a most unwise manner to one's lifetime of regrets and suffering."

"Yes, precisely so," says my master. "In fact, last autumn, a friend of mine was in that very infatuated state you just mentioned. But I am happy to tell you that I was able to save him from forming a most imprudent alliance. He was utterly smitten by this girl, who, I acknowledge, was indeed an uncommonly handsome girl with an engaging personality. But there were some very strong objections nonetheless against her circumstances, which should by no means be disregarded. Moreover, I was convinced that the girl's heart, though she welcomed his attentions with obvious gladness, was not struck by Cupid's arrow as his was. Had he married the girl, my friend would have regretted it in no time. He naturally suffered a great deal after he was separated from her, every day pining for her, which did make my heart ache for him. But a momentary suffering is better than a lifetime of regrets. I congratulate myself upon sparing my friend the harsh reality of the inevitable consequence."

"Your friend indeed was very lucky to have you," says the colonel.

I feel a little uneasy.

Should my master have told Colonel Fitzwilliam about his involvement in the separation of Mr Bingley and Miss Bennet? It is highly unlikely that the part my master played in the business will ever reach the ears of any persons concerned from the colonel's lips, but often the manner in which grapevines spread their tendrils is quite unpredictable and they have this annoying tendency to root themselves in the most unexpected, unwanted places. I hope no calamity will result from this.

* * * * *

We have arrived at Rosings Park, Lady Catherine de Bourgh's estate in Kent. It is not much more than twenty-five miles from London, and the journey has been quite comfortable.

If I be honest, I am not very fond of Lady Catherine. She is rather high in the instep, no, awfully high in the instep, and is an arrogant, overbearing and harsh-tempered termagant.

Chapter 12

She never has a single kind word to say to me, as if she thought we dogs are beneath her notice. I am at least allowed in her rooms, and for that I am thankful. But she does not suffer barks from me easily, though she often barks awfully herself. I have to sit still. If I run around or even let out a tiny woof, I will be in peril of being barked at.

She has this perpetually scowling, ill-tempered look on her face, except when she is fawned over. She is awfully fond of being revered and placed on a pedestal, and when she is flattered and attended with proper servility, she breaks into this exceedingly self-satisfied smile.

In some sense, she is a little like Miss Bingley. But the difference is that, while Miss Bingley is disdainful to whoever she thinks is beneath her and forever toadying to whoever is above her, Lady Catherine has not a bone in her body to be a sycophant herself to anyone. I cannot even for a moment picture her fawning over anybody. Her attitude does not change, as Miss Bingley's does, according to whom she is with. She would not pay deference, I could well imagine, even to the Price Regent himself. She would have that kind of gumption. I would at least say that for her.

My master and Colonel Fitzwilliam have refreshed themselves with the help no doubt of their respective valets (or perhaps Colonel Fitzwilliam's valet should be referred to as 'batman' in accordance with the Military custom?) after the rigours of travelling, and are now settled in the drawing room with Lady Catherine.

"You know, Darcy, Hunsford, the living I have in my gift?" says Lady Catherine to my master. "I have heard that you, while you were in Hertfordshire last autumn, made the acquaintance of Mr Collins, the rector there."

"Mr Collins? Yes, I believe I did," my master nods assent. "I thought him rather a ludicrous figure, an odd mixture of two contradictory traits, self-importance and obsequiousness."

"He does not seem at all odd to me," opines Lady Catherine, "He is a gratifyingly appreciative man, ever so sensitive to my infinite kindness to him and his people, and is always unstinting in showing his strong sense of gratitude for my patronage."

"I am glad that you have bestowed your munificence to so admirable a man who can recognize his good fortune and is not above demonstrating his gratefulness fully," says my master. I hear an unmistakable irony in his voice, but Lady Catherine does not seem to hear it at all.

"Oh, yes," ejaculates Lady Catherine. "I live for being kind and generous to my inferiors, and I oftentimes even suggest to them all kinds of useful hints and tit-bits for everyday life. You would be surprised to know just how lacking they are in common sense and basic knowledge of whatever it may be, how ignorant they are of things which are matters of course for such as ourselves. And when they show their due appreciation for my great kindness, I feel amply rewarded for my pains."

My master just nods to show he is at least listening, but seems unable to find any words to say. But Lady Catherine does not seem to mind, because she immediately proceeds.

"Even about something as important as marriage, they do not seem to be able to think themselves. For example, Mr Collins did not even begin to consider the matter of matrimony until I mentioned it. 'Mr Collins,' said I, 'you must marry. A clergyman like you must marry.' And I advised him to choose a gentlewoman not brought up too high, someone active, useful, and adept at household economy, and told him to find such a woman and bring her to Hunsford, and kindly promised him I would visit her."

My master again nods, signifying he is listening.

"And, what do you think?" Lady Catherine continues. "He did exactly what I had said he should do, and brought home a most suitable woman. I am informed that you made her acquaintance, too while you were in Hertfordshire. What, now, was her maiden name? Something beginning with L ... Yes, Lucas!"

"Lucas? Do you mean Miss Charlotte Lucas?" says my master, amazed.

"That is it! Charlotte. Charlotte Collins now."

Chapter 12

"It cannot be!" protests my master. "She seemed to have too much sense to be cozened into marrying such a ridiculous man!"

"You persist in saying Mr Collins is ridiculous. But he is nothing of the sort. He is a diligent, highly respectable man. Do not be silly. How can someone who appreciates me so well be ridiculous!"

Lady Catherine declaring thus with such authority, my master cannot say more.

"By the by, there is, at the moment at the personage, a visitor, or two visitors to be precise, whom you seem also to have been acquainted with in Hertfordshire. One is Miss Maria Lucas, Mrs Collins's sister and the other is Miss Elizabeth Bennet, Mrs Collins's close friend."

Miss Elizabeth!? I turn sharply to my master. With my acute sense of vision, I see my master visibly jump, though hopefully nobody else sees it. I see blood drain from my master's face first, then, gradually creep up dying his cheeks a little.

"Well, do you remember them?" lady Catherine demands.

My master, probably to collect himself, waits for some moments before he answers to his aunt's query.

"Miss Maria Lucas and Miss Elizabeth Bennet. Yes, I had the honour of their acquaintance," says my master, with admirably placid voice. He regains his composure at a most impressive speed as usual.

"You had the honour of their acquaintance? They had the honour of your acquaintance, you mean, surely?" Lady Catherine says.

My master smiles a wry smile at this remark of hers.

"No, I will not be so discourteous to ladies. It was I who had the honour," returns he.

"Well, in any event, as for this Miss Elizabeth Bennet, I hear that her father's entire estate will be, in the event of his demise, entailed away from the Bennets to Mr Collins, who is Mr Bennet's nearest male relative. It is, I acknowledge, a very good thing for Mr Collins, but I feel rather sorry for the daughters. I understand there are as many as five of them. It was really remiss of the parents not to have produced an heir. I strongly object to the notion of entail. A father's estate should all be bequeathed to his own offspring regardless of their sex. My Anne is truly fortunate in that sense, because she is to inherit everything as the sole heir though she is a female. You and Anne will be able to unite the two estates. What a good thing it is!"

Lady Catherine has set her mind on my master's forming an alliance with her daughter, Miss Anne de Bourgh, and at every possible opportunity refers to it. Miss de Bourgh blushes to the roots of her hair at her mother's allusion. My master always remonstrates to his aunt that he has no intention of making his cousin his wife, but he says nothing when his cousin is around for fear of hurting her feelings. Nevertheless, he remains mute, looking grim.

"Those Bennet girls," Lady Catherine continues, not heeding my master's accusing glances, "must find rich husbands if they are not to starve, but considering their lowly connections, it is not very likely."

At the mention of the Bennet girls' having to find husbands, I almost hear my master's heart jump.

As I did not have the opportunity to become personally acquainted with Mr Collins in Hertfordshire, I am quite interested to see the man, whom my master dismisses so freely as an oddity.

* * * * *

It is now the morning. Mr Collins with all alacrity has come to pay respects to the ladies and the gentlemen at Rosings, and I find he is indeed an oddity above any expectation. He has this tediously lengthy, exceedingly wordy way of speech, but I have not as yet seen any of the self-importance my master mentioned, but only obsequiousness.

To my master, Mr Collins seems to have especial respect to pay.

"My dear, dear, dear revered sir," so Mr Collins addresses my master, bowing almost comically low, "it is a great honour to be allowed to renew your acquaintance thus. It is indeed. What a great boon it will be to me and to my wife, who, I flatter myself, you will remember had the profoundest honour of your acquaintance last autumn in Hertfordshire, if we may be so honoured as to be allowed to receive you and your cousin, revered sirs, at my humble parsonage sometime at your earliest convenience. And I have two more people at my parsonage to whom, if I may, I would like to draw your attention. They are Miss Maria Lucas, my dear wife's sister, and Miss Elizabeth Bennet, my wife's best friend, who I am sure you will remember had also the great privilege of being known to you in Hertfordshire. They were kind enough to come and see how my wife was faring, and I am happy to be able to report to you that I am fully convinced that they are amply satisfied to see how fulfilling and pleasant a life my wife is leading here and how she enjoys the kind patronage of our most revered patroness, Lady Catherine de Bourgh, your saintly aunt."

In normal cases, in the middle of such a lengthy rigmarole of boring speech, my master would have given up listening, as my master is not a man to suffer fools gladly. But as Miss Elizabeth's name has been mentioned, he seems quite interested, lucky for Mr Collins.

Colonel Fitzwilliam, the courteous but easy-going and friendly gentleman that he is, is quite willing to oblige Mr Collins and to visit the parsonage with immediate effect.

My master must be quite willing, too, though of course he does not show it at all, and acquiesces with an impressively convincing guise of nonchalance.

* * * * *

So, thus, my master and Colonel Fitzwilliam accompany Mr Collins to his parsonage, and I, as a matter of course, follow them.

As the parsonage comes into view, Mr Collins runs ahead to forewarn the ladies. After a while, I hear woof-woof of a fellow canine and espy an Irish Setter running out of the parsonage, and I immediately recognize the familiar figure and the bark.

What a pleasant surprise this is! Dixon is here! Dixon, on the other hand, does not seem that surprised.

While the gentlemen go into the house and greet the ladies, I am allowed to have a little coze with Dixon in the fresh air outside.

"I have for some time known that we shall meet again," says Dixon, "as I found some time ago that your master was expected to be at Rosings soon on an established yearly Easter visit, and as I heard that your master always brings you, I have really been looking forward to meeting you again." And he gives me a friendly vigorous tail-wagging, and I return the same.

"So, why are you here?" I ask.

"Did you know Miss Lucas married Mr Collins?"

"I had not known until I arrived in Kent. So, she wished you to be with her in Kent, did she?"

"Yes. Of course, she had never been separated from her family before, and she seems to have felt very lonely at first when she started a new life here. I presume she wished to have some familiar face around her, so she wrote to my master asking him to allow her to keep me here. My master raised no objection whatsoever to parting with me. I should have been offended, but if I be honest, I was a poor excuse for a fowling dog, far from top-grade. I lacked the orderliness and methodicalness requisite for a gun-dog. I was a little too inquisitive. I tended to be too easily distracted by other things, and rather forgetting the object in view, wander off even during the hunt. And so, Miss Lucas – oh, pardon me, Mrs Collins, now – wishing me to come to Kent was a great adventure for me and tickled my fancy. I was most willing. And so, when my master and Miss Maria came to visit her this time, they brought me here."

"So, how did the marriage between Mr Collins and Miss Lucas come about?" I said. "I remember your once telling me, if I am not mistaken, that Mr Collins seemed to have his eye upon Miss Elizabeth when I was in Hertfordshire."

"Yes, he sure did. As a matter of fact, I heard he actually proposed to her, but she would not have him, and his pride was hurt though his heart was in no wise broken, wherein my mistress came to comfort him. And his injured pride was mollified, and things were settled to the satisfaction of all around them, except Mrs Bennet. I hear she was rather piqued that the two gentlemen whom she had thought were secured for her two eldests had both flown. I mean Mr Bingley and Mr

Collins. By the way, you know Miss Elizabeth is here, do you not?"

"Yes, when I heard Lady Catherine say so, I was so astonished, I nearly dropped my bone."

"Do you think your master still has feelings for her?

"I can confidently answer in the affirmative on that score. When my master heard from Lady Catherine that Miss Elizabeth was here, I could almost see and hear my master's heart stop and then start beating rapidly next. That is the sure sign that my master has still not forgotten her."

"Yes, hearing that Mr Darcy was coming to pay his respect at the parsonage so promptly, my mistress said it was all thanks to Miss Elizabeth, as high and mighty Mr Darcy would never have shown such civility to her."

"Did she, now? Then, your mistress is as perspicacious as ever," I say. "By the by, how did the matter go with regards to Mr Wickham back in Hertfordshire?" I ask.

"Oh, about that, Miss Elizabeth is safe from him," says he, "and, if I may say so myself, I had a lot to do with separating Miss Elizabeth from Mr Wickham. I am absolutely certain that you will commend me for my genius. Mr Wickham was, it was more than clear to everyone, 'sniffing after' Miss Elizabeth, if I may use that rather vulgar doggy colloquialism. To be frank, I did not know what to do, and in all honesty, there were times when I really feared I might not be able to protect Miss Elizabeth as I had promised, and you might think you placed your trust in me in vain.

"But one day, I chanced upon a great solution. I saw Miss Maria and her friends perusing a local ladies' magazine with uncommonly keen interest, and wondered what it was they were so avidly looking at. Then I overheard them say something about a small article about the news of Miss King's becoming an heiress, inheriting ten thousand pounds from an uncle. You might not have known her, but Miss King was a local girl, a pretty sort of girl, not too pretty, mind, who had been an ardent admirer of Mr Wickham, but who had not as yet managed to draw his attention to herself one whit. 'This is it! This will serve me perfectly!' I thought. I remembered you talking of Mr Wickham's great penchant for heiresses. As the magazine was a ladies' magazine, there was a great likelihood that Mr Wickham had not read or heard the news yet. Time was of the essence. I needed him to lose interest in Miss Elizabeth as soon as possible before he did any real damage. There was always a possibility that her heart might become engaged at any time. Without help from someone, it might take a long time for Mr Wickham to hear of Miss King's good fortune.

"Now, most fortuitously, there was to be a little gathering in Lucas Lodge that evening, and some neighbours and a few officers were to be invited, Mr Wickham amongst them. I devised a scheme. When everybody was gathered, I, with a perfect air of nonchalance, traipsed around the room and settled near Mr Wickham. I pretended to play with the magazine with the doggy-like insouciance, and after a while, just casually deposited it, with the pertinent page open, in front of Mr Wickham, where he could not but see it. I did everything I could to draw his attention to the article. Seeing Mr Wickham gazing at the article and afterwards seeming to be a little distracted as if thinking hard and plotting something, I could not help smiling to myself.

"And *voila*! Miss Elizabeth was thenceforward thrust aside, and he commenced a zealous courting and wooing of Miss King!"

I amend my notion that Dixon is not the cleverest of dogs. He is deuced impressive and has far exceeded my expectations! His ingenuity almost evokes awe! Even humans, who are forever boasting of being the most intelligent of species, I doubt, could have improvised such a scheme and carried it out so efficiently and efficaciously at such short notice.

* * * * *

My mind is easy as I have no cause to fear that anyone of Miss Bingley's calibre of persistence and daring will make an appearance suddenly to take my master unawares and get the better of him here. So I can leave him with Colonel Fitzwilliam, and go about my own business with clear conscience.

I, a gun-dog that I am, love roaming in wilderness, and often wander around on my own in vigorous exercise around the great expanse of the parks of Rosings.

On such occasions, I ever and anon come across Miss Elizabeth taking a tour of the park. She seems to be a very active lady, who needs almost as much exercise as I do. Her manner of walking is always brisk and jaunty, never dawdling, except when she stops to admire the flowers by the path-side which catch her eye. I always greet her with as much friendly sprightliness as possible. I am very anxious to give Miss Elizabeth a good, friendly impression, as I know my master fails in that sphere miserably.

I have long since noticed that it is a prevailing opinion among humans that dogs have a noted tendency to take on the characteristics of their masters and mistresses. And I am at my most charming, vivacious, amicable and lovable when I am with Miss Elizabeth, hoping that it might help to make Miss Elizabeth at least ponder upon the possibility that I have acquired those agreeable traits from being in close contact with my master, therefore, my master must be as friendly and jovial deep down as I am. The length and trouble I have to go to for my master's sake! I deserve far more than a bone or two! And this is not an idle conceit, but I am truly convinced that Miss Elizabeth considers me a deuced fine dog!

As my master has not the faintest clue how to recommend himself, it is always to others' lot that all the business of promoting his good qualities inevitably falls. Others have to think of everything and do everything on his behalf. And when I say 'others', I mean mainly me. But it is in no way an easy feat.

How does one recommend someone when that someone does not have the faintest clue how to make himself agreeable? If anyone has any idea, I should like to know.

☆ ☆ ☆ ☆ ☆

Chapter 12

While in Hertfordshire, my master forbade himself to fall deeper in Miss Elizabeth's thrall. Quitting Netherfield was partly to separate Mr Bingley from Miss Bennet, but I strongly suspect that separating himself from Miss Elizabeth figured even larger in his mind at the time. But the miniature kept his fond heart ever alive with Miss Elizabeth's image, and there was not a moment, as I am convinced, when he was free from the thought of her.

And after coming to Kent and being unexpectedly thrown thus into a situation where the reacquaintance with the lady is unavoidable, my master seems unable to suppress his feelings any more.

My master, too, has found that Miss Elizabeth regularly takes a walk around the park, and seems by some means to have also discovered which is her favoured route. I do not know how many times my master has so far succeeded in feigning coincidental encounters with her upon this route, but on this occasion I am here with them.

My master, as you know, is by no means a talkative man even at the best of times. With the lady of his heart in front of him, what little speech adroitness he possesses forsakes him and he becomes utterly useless. His tongue seems to become even more tightly tied in obstinate triple knots, and he walks on with her in absolutely 'uncompanionable' silence.

I endeavour to lift the atmosphere to lessen the damage. I run up to my master, sit in front of him and look up, wagging my tail, which causes him to kneel down and pat me as I have anticipated. I lick his cheek, which I well know from long experience will bring forth a kind of smile which not many people have seen him smile. And I can now clearly see that Miss Elizabeth is taken by surprise and is pretty impressed by my master's unexpectedly warm smile, which could be termed 'boyish', or even 'cute'. Well done me! I secretly congratulate myself.

If I could in this way show her many different aspects of my master so far seldom seen, she might begin to view my master in a totally different light.

Chapter 12

* * * * *

Whatever can be the cause for my master's fidgets? His nerves seem to be in a highly strung state, though I would not go so far as saying he is gnawing away at his nails as yet. He must be thinking of or even planning something momentous, some life changing event. Is he thinking of asking for Miss Elizabeth's hand in marriage? He has not mentioned any such intention in his daily mutterings to me, but I have that feeling, and feelings for us canines mean more than just feelings. They could even be termed as 'prescience'.

* * * * *

It does seem my master is seriously considering asking Miss Elizabeth to be his wife. But that does not mean he has definitely made up his mind. I can see he is still debating whether or not that is really the path he should take.

* * * * *

Today again, my master has sought Miss Elizabeth during her daily tour of the park, and now they are walking side by side with me as their companion as before.

I cannot quite tell from Miss Elizabeth's countenance whether she is pleased or displeased with my master thus repeatedly chancing (in a manner of speaking) upon her on her walks, but that she is rather puzzled by it, is written all over her face.

My master on this occasion is making an unprecedented effort to be conversant.

"Eh, Miss Bennet," he begins a conversation, "I noticed as early as when I was still in Hertfordshire that you were very fond of taking walks, enjoying fresh air."

"Oh, yes, I am very much one who prefers outdoor activities to more sedate indoor occupation. I am afraid that it must be deemed rather unfashionable. Mr Bingley's sisters would never have approved of me.

Chapter 12

And neither would you, I imagine," says Miss Elizabeth. Do I sense a slight hint of irony in it?

"You judge me totally wrong, Miss Bennet," my master defends himself. "I think parks and countryside are there to be enjoyed from within as well as from without. I do very much approve of your favouring outdoor activities and fresh air."

"Oh ... thank you," says Miss Elizabeth somewhat lamely as if the wind has been taken out of her sails.

"Eh, so, I trust you have had as many opportunities as you like to enjoy the grounds of Rosings since you came to Kent?"

"Oh, yes, thank you. The weather has been excellent, and allowed me to come out for a walk every day. Vast as the parks may be, I have gained quite an extensive knowledge of how the grounds lie. I have become, I should imagine, quite an authority," says Miss Elizabeth in a pleasant joking tone.

"You have visited the house often as well, I trust?"

"Ah, yes, but of that, I cannot at all claim to have gained an extensive knowledge! Every time I visit the house, I all but lose my way. Even the corridors just from the entrance hall to the drawing room are so complex and labyrinthine that I wonder how people can ever find their way. I have never thought myself lacking in sense of direction, but I am beginning to think I am."

"Ah, no, it has nothing to do with your sense of direction. The late Sir Louis de Bourgh and many of his predecessors were quite avid reorganisers of the house, and Rosings has been altered, extended, new wings built and demolished. As a result, the layout of the interior is rather convoluted, and not quite what you would normally expect," thus my master explains.

"Oh, is that so? It means I will just have to become accustomed to the place by and by."

"Perhaps, next time you visit Kent, you may find yourself at Rosings not as a mere casual visitor, but more in the capacity of an insider, and may be given ample opportunities to do so," says my master.

That was a very bold hint at his intentions.

Chapter 12

Miss Elizabeth looks not a little puzzled and flustered. Has she understood his meaning? I cannot say she seems particularly excited, but she does not look as if she disliked it, either.

Chapter 12

Chapter 13

In which my master encounters the most severe trial in his life

As usual, I roam in the park. The day is most salubrious. The easterly wind has turned a little southerly, and when I raise my head high and sniff the air, I can smell the distinct scent of spring.

A little ahead, I descry the tall figure of Colonel Fitzwilliam, who is taking the tour of the park as he always does towards the end of his Easter visit to his aunt's each year. I look for my master, who accompanies his cousin on these yearly walks as a normal practice, but I do not see him on this occasion.

I follow the same route as Colonel Fitzwilliam, thinking my master might converge upon him any time.

When we walk a little farther on, I espy a dainty figure of a lady approaching us from the other direction, and I instantly recognize Miss Elizabeth. She is walking unusually slowly in comparison with her customary pace, due, it seems, to her being absorbed in perusing a letter while walking.

Colonel Fitzwilliam and I walk up to her, but Miss Elizabeth does not seem to become aware of our approach till we are up close.

Colonel Fitzwilliam hails her in his usual voice of easy friendliness, and Miss Elizabeth looks up. Does my keen sense of vision detect a slight hint of regret flit across her face as if she wished she could continue the perusal of the letter? But that slight hint of regret immediately passes before it could possibly be seen by the colonel, and Miss Elizabeth's face burgeons into an welcoming smile.

A mundane greetings are exchanged and upon the colonel saying he means to call at the parsonage to close the tour of the park, she agrees to return there together, and they start in the direction of the parsonage. I follow them.

I suddenly become conscious of an unsettling, jittery feeling without any apparent reason, some sort of a presentiment ...

"So, you and Mr Darcy are to leave the day after tomorrow?" Miss Elizabeth says.

"Yes, if Darcy does not alter his mind and postpone it again," the colonel answers. "I am at his mercy. He has changed his mind twice already, which is a deuced rare thing, as he is as a rule not a man prone to vacillate."

I know the cause of my master's vacillation. He could not make up his mind regarding Miss Elizabeth and was dragging it out, not being able to bolster up his courage. But I now know that he has finally made a firm resolve to ask her hand in marriage – tomorrow.

Upon this comment of Colonel Fitzwilliam's, Miss Elizabeth says something about my master's being a man to derive enormous pleasure from having the power to control others and elaborates upon it a great deal, which I think is rather unfair and shows that her opinion of my master regrettably has not much improved for all my pains.

Their conversation gradually passes from there to Miss Darcy, then to Mr Bingley. And Miss Elizabeth says something about my master taking great care of the gentleman. Every time she mentions my master, her voice seems to carry some tone of censure or irony, and I groan with a sinking feeling.

Chapter 13

Then, horror of horrors, a great disaster strikes!

Colonel Fitzwilliam makes a reference to my master's having saved Mr Bingley from a most imprudent marriage! Oh, I knew this would happen! Of course the blame cannot be laid at the colonel's door, as there is no reason why he should have guessed that the lady concerned was Miss Elizabeth's sister. My master should have warned him, or what would have been better still, he should never have divulged it at all even to the colonel.

The colonel does not seem to see anything is at all amiss, but I sense at once every line of Miss Elizabeth's body become taut and rigid, and her jaw line stiffen, and I definitely smell her profound displeasure!

Their discourse afterwards upon this topic, to my great perturbation, seems to place my master in a more and more disadvantageous light, and I know Miss Elizabeth is growing yet further aggravated.

Ah, this is why I have always been worried. I hoped that my fear that nothing good comes from interfering with other people's love was groundless but it has proven to be well-founded. Woe never fails to betide those who meddle with other people's love.

* * * * *

The parsonage people are come to take tea at Rosings as planned but Miss Elizabeth is not with them. Mrs Collins gives a severe headache as the reason for her absence. I steal a glance at my master, and see an unmistakable expression of disappointment unusually perceivable cross his face.

Is her headache a mere excuse or real, and if real, has it been brought on by her anger, exasperation, and even hatred against my master? Will she ever forgive him? Will she be able to forget it given time? I feel useless. I am a mere canine. What can I ever do to ameliorate the situation?

This anguish suddenly makes me desirous to pass water. Of course, I have not done so for several hours now, so it is about time in any event. I discreetly let myself out of the room without drawing attention to myself, then head for outside, and successfully relieve myself.

Maybe, I should remain outside for a while longer to let them enjoy tea without the presence of a canine while they do so.

I ponder upon the problem of Miss Elizabeth's ire while I wander thus outside and wait for the right moment to go in. One thing is certain. This is decidedly not the right time for my master to take the plunge and go ahead with his proposing. If he does so tomorrow, the outcome can only be disastrous. But how can I convey this to my master? I will be able to show my disapprobation by grabbing hold of a part of my master's garment with my teeth, and refusing to let him go to Miss Elizabeth. I know such will be the only method that I will be able to take ...

I spend about half to three quarters of an hour outside cogitating thus. Then, deciding it is about time to return, I let myself in from the side entrance and go to the drawing room. Upon entering the room, I immediately note my master's absence. Where has he gone? I have a dreadful feeling.

I rush out of the drawing room and look into the water closet just in case. No, he is not there. What about the library? No, not there, either. Has he gone back to his own bedchamber? I run up the stairs, with that dreadful feeling perpetually pursuing me, but hoping against hope that my master is in his chamber.

I rush into my master's room and all but collide into Mr Trent who is just leaving the room. I run around the chamber, but there is no sign of my master.

I make haste and run out into the corridor again and bark, circling around Mr Trent, hoping he would take my meaning that I wish to know my master's whereabouts.

"Now now, take care, Julius Caesar!" says he. "Are you looking for your master? He is not here, nor is he in his study. Surely, he is in the drawing room, is he not?"

There is no time to lose. Without even one woof to signify my gratitude to Mr Trent, which discourtesy I hope he will look leniently upon, I run down the corridor, down the stairs, and rush out of the house.

I run as fast as I have never done before, hanging onto a small sliver of hope that my master has not reached the parsonage yet, at the same time however, feeling in my bones that I am much too late.

I arrive at the parsonage and I frantically run around the house, to discover which room my master and Miss Elizabeth are in. I see light emanating from the French windows of the parlour at the rear, and rush towards them.

I feel my stomach drop to the pads of my feet.

I see my master standing near the fireplace, his face grim, but with a certain stunned expression in it. Miss Elizabeth has her back towards me, so I am unable to see her expression, but in the line of her shoulders, in the angle she holds her head, and in the tone of her voice which I can, though only faintly, hear through the panes of the closed French windows, I sense her anger, displeasure and intransigent hostility towards my master.

I see Dixon sitting in the corner of the room, earnestly listening, and understand that he has seen me, too. I have to hear the full account of this business from him later.

Soon, my master bows to Miss Elizabeth stiffly to take his leave. His outward mien is collected and unperturbed, but I, who have known him intimately and know every sign of the state, process and workings of his inner emotions, recognise how thoroughly devastated and beaten he is.

I wish to go to my master and console him, but I do not know if it is the best thing to do. Maybe, my master needs sometime alone, as we dogs, when we are injured, sometimes wish to go hiding for a little while to lick our wounds.

I suspect that Dixon intends to come out after my master to have a talk with me, so I shall wait here for him to come and find me.

Now, here is Dixon!

"Dear Julius Caesar!" says Dixon. "Commiserations to your master. He has received a severe dressing down, and his suit has been rejected in the cruellest of terms. What is this about your master ruining the happiness of Miss Elizabeth's sister?"

"Ah, so Miss Elizabeth did mention it, did she? Well ... "

And I relate briefly the business of my master separating Mr Bingley from Miss Bennet, and the colonel inadvertently blurting it out to Miss Elizabeth this morning.

"That was damned unfortunate!" says Dixon.

"But Dixon, were you there from the beginning, from the time my master first entered the room?" Dixon nods. "I wish to hear it all. All that has transpired. How did my master first address Miss Elizabeth?"

"Ah, Julius Caesar, your master, I am fully informed, is a very intelligent man, and yet, he does not seem to have any clue about how to treat a woman or what will please a woman! Absolutely no clue whatever!"

"Oh, you do not have to tell me that. I know it perfectly well. I have been his companion for three and a half years now, do you not know? How many times have I groaned with worry, impatience, desperation, and despair for my master and secretly cursed his ways which seem to be designed to offend and alienate others rather than to please them? But, how did my master proceed with his suit? Please tell me."

"Well, he first paced about the room for a few moments in an agitated fashion most unlike his normal self, then came up to where Miss Elizabeth was seated, and poured forth his feelings for her, how he had loved and admired her from the very dawn of their acquaintance and such, and asked her to accept his hand in marriage. So far so good."

"By that, I presume, you mean the rest was a steady downhill."

"Precisely so. Utterly dismal. After that initial love declaration, what your master dwelt upon next to a great length was his sense of doing himself and those who belonged to him great wrong and injustice by pursuing such an unequal alliance."

I close my eyes and let out a long groan. What lady would not have been offended by such an address!?

Chapter 13

"Then, Miss Elizabeth, who must have been seething inside, said in a surprisingly collected voice nonetheless, that the normal mode of practice in such a situation must be that she should convey her sense of gratitude for the offer. But, she solemnly continued, she could not. Your master visibly flinched at that. A plucky lady that she is, she told your master in the clearest terms that she had never wished for his good opinion, which he had obviously vouchsafed upon her most grudgingly in any event, and politely but firmly, with quite a hint of irony, she rejected the suit."

"And that, I suppose, was not the end of the matter."

"No, no, far from it. Your master, manifestly riled at being so offhandedly rejected, most unwisely inquired why he had been rejected with so little endeavour at civility. In my opinion, your master made a very unwise choice of words, as he had been a far cry from being civil himself in his mode of proposing. And of course, she latched onto that fact and retorted with a sharp tongue, referring precisely to his own incivility. Which she said, however, was not the only inducement to her bad opinion of him. And that was when she mentioned Miss Bennet and her hopes for happiness brought to wrack and ruin by your master."

"And how did my master behave, then? Was he contrite?"

"Contrite!? Contrite!? No, far from it! He was anything but contrite! He said he rejoiced in his success, and even added that he had been kinder to Mr Bingley than to himself!"

Damn and blast! I let out an even longer groan.

"Humans, my dear Julius Caesar," Dixon continues to remark, "are supposed to be gifted with far greater intelligence than any other species, but they so often behave as if they were with pates as hollow as those of scarecrows. If even your master, who is considered by many to be a real intellectual, could behave in so silly a fashion, what hope would there be for imbeciles?"

And I cannot fault this observation, either. Dixon seems to be growing wiser by the day!

"Thoroughly angered by this remark of your master's, Miss Elizabeth set out to launch an offensive. Do you know, Julius Caesar, Mr Wickham seems really to have been a villain of the first order. He must have told the grossest lies to sully your master's name. What Miss Elizabeth said next clearly indicated that Mr Wickham had provided her with some mendacious story about your master having acted dishonourably in some capacity in the past, which was the direct cause for Mr Wickham's present predicament and penury."

"And Miss Elizabeth believed it, believed my master could ever behave in a dishonourable way! Frailty, thy name is woman! See a handsome face, and she believes in anything the man says ... But, wait. On second thoughts, the fault also lies with my master. I cannot deny that my master has not the pleasant, handsome address of Mr Wickham, and the overall impression of my master is that he is haughty and aloof at the best, and he has done nothing to alter that impression, or try and cultivate his manners to a more attractive and engaging level."

"Maybe, your master has had no occasion so far which called for such endeavour. Ladies must have flocked thick and fast around him without any efforts on his part."

"That is true, but it is no excuse all the same."

"Anyway, to continue the story, when Miss Elizabeth thus showed her great concern for Mr Wickham's welfare and accused your master of having been the evil bringer of Mr Wickham's ruin, your master seemed greatly angered, perturbed and saddened by the unjust imputation. I could have said he was positively jealous as well. The hurt and jealousy, in a manner of speaking, must have made him retaliate in a rather disdaining fashion and reiterate Miss Elizabeth's inferior station in social standing. He said that, grave as his offence might have been in her eyes, she might have overlooked it, had her pride not been hurt by his honest feelings about her inferior station. He demanded to know if she could have expected him to rejoice in her low connections. In consequence of this harangue, he made Miss Elizabeth even angrier. Miss Elizabeth's retort was to the effect that it had been many months since she had decided that your master was a most disagreeable man and she would never consider marrying such as he even if there were no other men left in the world."

"By Jove, that was harsh, downright pitiless!"

"Wasn't it just!?"

* * * * *

I run back to Rosings. I visit the drawing room first, where the guests from the parsonage are still gathered, but as I have been expecting, I do not find my master there. I scuttle up the stairs and hurry to his bedchamber. I stop in front of his door and listen. No sound whatsoever can I hear from within. I push the door open quietly and enter the room to see my master sprawled upon the bed, with his gaze fixed at the thick canopy of the bed above. I walk up to the bed, the pads of my feet making a soft patter upon the floor.

Hearing the pitter-patter of my feet, my master turns his head. The expression in his eyes almost halts me in my tracks. Never have I seen them so forlorn, so devastated, or so tortured.

My master scrambles himself up to the sitting position. His hair, which usually is fashionably styled, is now completely tousled, denoting that he has been rumpling and tugging at it. I jump onto the bed, which is a particular indulgence my master allows me. Without a word, my master pulls me to him and hugs me ever so tightly, nearly knocking the breath out of my lungs, and mutters to me, "Julius Caesar, Miss Elizabeth will not have me. She said I was the last man upon earth that she could be prevailed upon to consent to marry." Then he buries his face deep into my fur. After a while, to my utter horror, my master's body starts to convulse with silent sobs. The sheer weight of his grief is felt in the hotness of the tears flowing into my fur.

The sob subsides at last, but my master remains in the same position for a long time afterwards, his face still buried in my fur.

But after the long silence, he raises his head, rubs his face vigorously and slaps it a few times with the palms of his hands as if to whip himself up, and then, he pats my head, I presume, as a token of his appreciation of my contribution, before he rises from the bed and strides to the wash table to pour water from the pitcher into the wash basin. He splashes the cold water onto his face several times, never heeding the water cascading down his shirt's front.

"Now, I am done!" says he. "How abjectly unmanly it was of me to weep in that fashion! Such weakness is absolutely derisible, is it not, Julius Caesar!? Wickham – that infernal scoundrel, that godless villain – must have supplied Miss Elizabeth with all and sundry falsehood about me. I shall have to write to her, laying bare all the facts. Damned if I let that reptile of a man get away with such a gross misdemeanour!"

So, my master is for the time being recovered from his fit of the dismals. While the thought of exonerating himself of the ignominy, which Mr Wickham perfidiously ascribed to him, is riding high in his priorities, his spirits will remain supported. But how long this brave outlook will last is not certain. When my master has written the letter to Miss Elizabeth explaining all the particulars that need to be explained, and his days return to the routine before this heartbreak, he will feel the pain afresh again. Of that I am certain.

* * * * *

My master has had a fitful sleep. Dawn is still a long time to come, but my master has risen from bed and seems to have decided to commence writing the intended letter to Miss Elizabeth. He dips the quill in the inkwell and begins to write. At first the pen does not at all seem to flow, but after he has managed to write a few laborious lines, it seems to begin gaining momentum.

He is now scratching away at the paper apace. It appears that it is going to be a deuced long letter.

* * * * *

The letter is now written, and my master is fixing the wax to seal it.

Turning to me with a very faint forlorn smile upon his face, my master says, “Now, Julius Caesar, it is done. All that is left for me to do is to endeavour to find Miss Elizabeth and place this letter in her custody.”

* * * * *

As the time of Miss Elizabeth's daily walk approaches, my master becomes restless. He begins to pace the room. Walking back and forth, back and forth, rather reminiscent of a bear in captivity which I have once seen, my master now and again steals a glance at the clock upon the mantelpiece.

“Now, it is time to go,” my master says, and strides out of the room, and as usual I follow suit.

* * * * *

The letter has been given to Miss Elizabeth.

Miss Elizabeth is an intelligent lady, and is also, I am fully persuaded, a fair-minded person, who could distinguish facts from falsehood when both are presented to her in juxtaposition. Formerly, she had access to falsehood alone provided by that villain, Wickham, and not to any of the facts, and when one cannot weigh one against the other, it is very difficult to judge.

I hope, dearly hope, that my master's letter will make short work thereof.

Chapter 13

Chapter 14

In which I do my utmost to ameliorate the situation

My master has come to the parsonage to bid them adieu and I have followed him, too, as we are leaving Kent tomorrow morning. I do not know whether or not my master has been hoping for a last sight of Miss Elizabeth, but the question is moot as she is not here. It is already nearly two hours since my master handed her the letter, but she has still not returned. She must be roaming about the park, trying to digest my master's letter.

I, too, bid adieu, a reluctant adieu, to Dixon. I do not know when I will be able to see him again, most likely not till next year.

My master has returned to Rosings but, I have decided to search for Miss Elizabeth to see how the waters now lie in that quarter.

I roam around Miss Elizabeth's haunts, and after a while, espy the lady leaning against a large oak tree, studying my master's letter. She seems rather agitated and repeats the process of folding the letter and putting it away, then taking it out and unfolding it to read, time and time again.

I run up to her. She sees me, and smiling a little wanly without her usual vivacity, kneels down to hug me as usual. I am very eager to find out whether her feelings towards my master have undergone some change.

"Ah, Julius Caesar, I see that your master is not with you. I am truly relieved," says she.

Oh, then, does she still hold my master in abhorrence? Has the letter not produced the wished-for effect? I feel bitterly disappointed.

But then, "I have not the tranquillity of mind to see your master," she continues to say. "His letter has overturned all that I was led to believe, and I do not know what to think. At first, I could not credit it at all, but now after many a careful perusal, I cannot but come to a conclusion that it was not Mr Wickham who was the injured party, but your master. Could I really have I been so unjust? Did I think I was certain of everything when I was actually certain of nothing? Has your master been really blameless? Oh, I do not know! And yet, it must be so, because everything points to that direction. There is many a thing which I did not think strange at all before, but which, now after reading your master's missive, I see in a completely different light."

I turn my eyes to heaven and thank the Lord.

"And even about Mr Bingley and my sister," Miss Elizabeth continues to muse, "I now understand that Mr Darcy is not the only one to blame. Of course, it does not alter the fact that he is still a proud man and not altogether agreeable, but that is not for me to judge."

A proud man and not altogether agreeable ... Of course, for that, my master has only himself to blame.

* * * * *

Before I leave Rosings, I have to do something. I should at least devise some way to let Miss Elizabeth know how truly my master has loved her and for how long. The only means I can think of is the miniature. It clearly shows that the likeness was taken at the Netherfield Ball. If Miss Elizabeth could somehow be induced to see that miniature, she would realize that my master was already deeply in love with her at such an early stage of their acquaintance, which surely would gratify her now that she seems a little mollified and appears to be beginning to feel a trifle kinder towards my master.

Everybody is now taking tea, and my absence will not be noted. I hurry to my master's study. I know where he keeps his miniature – in the bottom drawer of his writing bureau. Opening a drawer is a little tricky business, but not as tricky as turning a key. The drawer is very well waxed and slides out in perfect smoothness. The miniature is placed in a pouch with a string which tightens the opening. I fish out the pouch by the string with my mouth. I am about to slide the draw in, and then, I happen to see a letter. It is the one Colonel Fitzwilliam mentioned in the carriage upon the way to Kent – the letter Mr Wickham wrote to my master, acknowledging the receipt of the three thousand pounds! I think swiftly. If I could show this letter to Miss Elizabeth, surely she will understand that my master has never treated Mr Wickham in an dishonourable way. Three thousand pounds is an enormous sum, almost an astronomical sum for such as Mr Wickham. She will know that Mr Wickham has only himself to blame for his present penury.

I pick up the letter, too. I push in the drawer, which slides back in even more smoothly than when I slid it out.

I carry the pouch of the miniature and the letter in my mouth, taking great care not soil them with my saliva, and run to the parsonage.

I again circle around the house to discover which room the parsonage people are in. If possible, I wish to find Dixon first, as he will be of great help. I see Miss Elizabeth in the back parlour again. Mrs Collins is there with her, but Miss Maria Lucas is nowhere to be seen. Dixon immediately notices me. Very shortly, Mrs Collins rises from her seat and fortuitously leaves the room in all probability in order to supervise something.

As a result, Miss Elizabeth is left alone, which must pose a capital opportunity for me. Dixon comes to the French windows and scratches them rather loudly. Unlike me, he has not yet mastered the art of opening doors, so he needs to attract Miss Elizabeth's attention. The scratching noise Dixon has made draws Miss Elizabeth's eyes to the French windows, and she sees me standing outside. A smile spreads upon her face, which makes me feel that her feelings towards my master have improved yet further, and I hope it is not my deluded, wishful thinking. Miss Elizabeth opens the French windows and out comes Dixon, to whom I hurriedly explain why I have come.

Miss Elizabeth kindly invites me in, and I take this good opportunity to draw her attention to the pouch which contains the all-important miniature, and the letter which also contains the all-important history of the transaction between my master and Mr Wickham.

I play with the pouch and the letter first in a nonchalant, playful-doggy fashion to plant the notion firmly into Miss Elizabeth's mind that I have brought them just by some doggy accident. Next, I place them on her lap, still pretending to be playing with them, and then, sit in front of her, expectantly looking up at her.

Miss Elizabeth, looking a little puzzled, takes the letter up.

"Whatever can it be?" she says, and unfolds it. "Oh, my God! This is a private letter from Mr Wickham to Mr Darcy! I cannot possibly read it!" she cries, and folds it up again.

Damn! I hope she will do away with such a rigid notion! I patiently wait. She fidgetingly fiddle with the letter. Maybe her curiosity will get the better of her.

As if deciding she cannot suppress her curiosity any longer, she hurriedly opens the letter again, and reads.

"Oh, this is exactly what Mr Darcy said in his letter! Three thousand pounds! Such a fortune! And yet, Mr Wickham falsely claimed Mr Darcy had treated him dishonourably. And moreover, the letter also mentions some other former occasions when Mr Darcy had reached out a helping hand to Mr Wickham. Mr Darcy must have always been so generous to Mr Wickham."

She folds the letter again slowly, and seems to be in deep thoughts. After a while, she starts as if she had snapped out of reverie.

She, then, remembers the pouch, opens it and looks in. Looking at me with inquiry in her eyes, she takes out the miniature. In spite of myself, my heart pounds while I await her reaction.

She looks at the miniature, and her eyes open wide.

"This is ... well, so unexpected," utters Miss Elizabeth. "I never knew my likeness was taken. When can it have been? Was it at the Netherfield Ball? This dress ... I am sure I did not wear it on any other occasion. Has your master kept it all this time?"

I see a manifest softening in the expression of her eyes, which my master has once most aptly called fine, and congratulate myself upon the brilliant piece of work.

Miss Elizabeth, naturally, has no notion whatsoever that I have brought the miniature and the letter to her with a definite objective in mind. Her natural assumption, I imagine, must be that it is nothing but a coincidence that I have done so. In her eyes, I am but a pet dog without much intellect, who does not know what he is doing. Though like my master, she makes a habit of talking to me when she is with me, she, of course, never expects me to understand much, if anything.

"You must have inadvertently taken these items from somewhere, which you should not have done. You are a very naughty doggy. You must carry them back to your master without a mishap," says Miss Elizabeth, patting my back as she usually does. She returns the miniature to the pouch, then puts the letter into the pouch, too, and to my horror, fixes the string of the pouch to my dog collar!

Damnation! I shall have a hell of a difficulty in taking it off, if indeed it is at all possible!

* * * * *

Oh, God, God, God! No! I cannot take it off! It will stubbornly refuse to be eased out of the knot! Oh, dear! I cannot risk being seen by my master with this blasted pouch hanging from my dog collar! He will wonder how it has come to be fixed there!

Calm down. Let's think this through carefully. Now, what can I do to get out of this mess? My only salvation, if there is one, must lie in the

Chapter 14

person of Mr Trent. He is the only human being that suspects anything of my intellectual capacity, if not anywhere near the full extent – indeed, who would?

I head for Mr Trent's room, hoping I will not run into my master upon the way. When I have reached the landing, I hear my master calling me from down below, but I do not heed him. I run like mad and tear my way into Mr Trent's room, where, however, I do not find him. Hearing a faint noise in my master's room through the wall, I rush into the room and find Mr Trent brushing my master's coat. I grab hold of Mr Trent's sleeve and with all my might drag him back into his own room, and slam shut his door.

Now, I have to let him see the pouch under my jaw.

I raise my jaw, and indicate the pouch as clearly as my awkward paw can do the office.

For a few moments, Mr Trent does not notice the pouch, but then, his eyes are finally drawn to it.

”Now, now, Julius Caesar, what mischief have you been getting up to this time with that miniature?” he says with a raised brow. As if I were always getting up to mischief like the incorrigible imp, Puck!

I try to tug at the pouch to show him that I wish it to be released from my collar. Mr Trent seems to capture my meaning swiftly and obliges me. Soon, the pouch is safely detached from my dog collar.

“What is this? Something else is in the pouch,” says Mr Trent, and opens it and sees the letter, too. Taking out the letter from the pouch, “What in heaven's name have you been doing with this letter?” he says, in a completely flummoxed tone.

Just at that moment, I hear the door from the corridor to my master's room open, and then my master's voice call out my name. I fall in a panic. He will at any moment come to Mr Trent's door and open it!

I think quickly, pick the pouch and the letter up with my mouth, and rush under Mr Trent's bed. With luck, Mr Trent will not betray where I am, and if he does, I just have to come out, that is all. One thing is for certain, though. Mr Trent will not betray a thing about the miniature pouch and the letter, as he does not know the particulars concerning how they had got to be attached to my dog collar, and while he has not the faintest clue how, he will not mention it, because he will not dare risk my master thinking it was his doing.

I hear the sound of Mr Trent's door opening, and then my master's voice say, "Trent, is Julius Caesar here? I saw him run up the stairs and come this way, but he is not in my bedchamber. Why, Julius Caesar, my boy, what are you doing under Trent's bed!?"

Damn! What has given me away!? Oh, yes, the tip of my tail must have been showing! I drop the pouch and the letter in the deep shadow at the far end so that they could not be seen even if my master should happen to peer under the bed, and then, back out in a little undignified manner.

I rush to my master and run around him, pretending to be really excited, to divert his attention from whatever my master might think I have been doing under the bed. Then I hurry out of the room, knowing my master will follow me and I will be out of the perilous situation. I have absolutely no doubt in my mind that Mr Trent will fetch the offending pouch and the letter out from under the bed and return them safely to the bottom drawer of my master's writing bureau at the earliest opportunity.

* * * * *

Now, we are leaving Rosings.

When the carriage trundles past the narrow lane which leads to the parsonage, a shadow descends upon my master's face. Oh, how he must be feeling the wrench of parting!

Chapter 14

Chapter 15

In which we travel to London, where my master attends the Season, during which he is assailed by not just Miss Bingley, but three more determined damsels

We are back in Town. It is the height of London Season now and the capital is alive with the *ton* who are back from their country seats, intent upon thrusting and hoisting their sons and daughters of marriageable ages onto the stage of the marriage mart.

My master, I fear, will be mobbed by many a débutante, many a lady of not so tender an age who has been on the market for some years, and many a matron with a daughter hunting for a husband alike. And to make matters even worse, my master is in a most wretched state.

Just as I predicted, my master is feeling the pain afresh as his days return to the former routine. He becomes tormented by the memories of Miss Elizabeth, her angry face, her harsh words, and her rejection.

Especially in that brief period of quiescence in the evening between the hustle and bustle of daytime activities and the time the *ton* begin to prepare for the night's entertainments, when twilight gradually gathers stealing across the streets of London and hours seem most poignant, my master is most wretched.

Oh, how I wish I could tell him that Miss Elizabeth hates him no more, that his letter, his miniature, and Mr Wickham's letter, have dissolved her prejudice, and set his mind at rest!

He now sits with me with his arms around me.

"I often hear people preach, Julius Caesar," my master mutters to my ear with his head upon the back of my neck and nuzzling into my hair, as if to draw consolation from the warmth of my body, "that the period during which one nurses one's unrequited love is the best time of one's life. But I think it is complete pish and tosh."

I certainly think it is complete pish and tosh, too, judging from my master's state now.

"But fair to say," my master continues, "it is what one thinks, I suppose, when one looks back upon such a time afterwards. Then, and only then, one could reminisce and say, 'Ah those were truly fruitful, formative years!' I dearly hope I shall, too, some day be able to reminisce upon this anguish with a little more poise."

I trust to providence that everything may come right for my master in the end.

* * * * *

It is entirely out of the question for me to accompany my master to any of the *ton*'s events.

According to the scraps of information I have garnered from divergent sources – such as talks between Mr Bingley and Mr Hurst, discourses between my master and his friends, confabulations between Miss Bingley and Mrs Hurst, gossips flying about among the servants below stairs ... – there seem to be at least three ladies who are pursuing my master with such zeal as to draw people's attention. A Lady Cilia Chattaway, a Miss Isabella Throttlebottom, and a Miss Sarah Wiggles-Pennyworth ... No wonder, methinks, they cannot wait to marry. But I would have thought they would not mind who they marry, never mind the best on the market, as long as they can rid themselves of ridiculous surnames like these.

And it goes without saying that Miss Bingley has no intention whatsoever of retiring from the matrimonial race gracefully. Miss Bingley alone would have been a big enough problem, but how my master is expected to cope with four determined damsels is a question that I am unable to solve and do not even wish to ponder upon. So, not only does my head ache, but my stomach churns with worry. Moreover, as I have said, my master has suffered that great psychological blow, and is not quite himself. He is in a precarious state of ennui and could easily be taken advantage of.

But where I secretly place the best hopes is that those four ladies, in their desperate endeavour to outdo others and to hinder and counter each other's moves and progresses, will inadvertently act as perfect foils for my master as effective as no other, enabling him to parry their attacks.

* * * * *

Mr Bingley, Miss Bingley and the Hursts are the honoured guests at the dinner at my master's London residence today.

I happen to pass by one of the rooms allocated to the guests where they could get themselves ready before going down for dinner.

The room, I believe, is allotted to Miss Bingley and I can hear the conversation between her and her sister.

"I have been quite put out, Louisa," says Miss Bingley to her sister, "by the shabby manner in which I am constantly served by Lady Chattaway, Miss Trottlebottom and Miss Wiggles-Pennyworth!"

"How do you mean?" says Mrs Hurst.

"Oh, you know, do you not, that they set their sights firmly upon Mr Darcy, and never leave him alone! They flock around him constantly and I can never find time but when at least two of them are fawning over Mr Darcy, batting their eyelashes, fluttering their fans, and giggling in a ridiculously coquettish fashion. Indeed, it is so very tiresome! They seem to be trying to prevent my every move! They are terribly, terribly in my way. Do they not know that they are not wanted?"

"You should get in their way in your turn," suggests Mrs Hurst.

"Oh, you need not worry," replies Miss Bingley. "I have been totally vigilant. For example, at Mrs Carstairs' musical soirée the other day, I strongly suspected that Isabella Throttlebottom and Lady Cilia were scheming to secure a seat next to Mr Darcy as soon as he came and found a seat. So, I waylaid them and engaged them in some discourse in the aisle so that they could not proceed to do so when Mr Darcy arrived. But annoyingly, I, too, failed to secure a seat next to Mr Darcy, as, while I was thus trying to distract their attention, Mr Darcy came and sat, and both the adjacent seats were immediately taken by some others before I even realized it. Oh, it was so very vexing!"

"Oh, poor dear!" says Mrs Hurst consolingly.

"And only last night," continues Miss Bingley, "when Mr Darcy was surrounded by other people, I firmly stationed myself by the side of him as I knew he would abhor any other lady to be near him. But that odious Sarah Wiggles-Pennyworth would not have it and endeavoured to squeeze in between Mr Darcy and me in a most undignified fashion! The audacity of it! It was absolutely shocking!"

"I hope you did not let her have her way."

"Oh, of course not! As if I would! I glared at her, and said, 'Would you mind?' in as frosty and disdainful a tone as I could assume. But that chit was so brazen. She did not even blush with shame!"

"Indeed!? Young ladies these days!" cries Mrs Hurst.

"Yes, is it not appallingly outrageous!?" says Miss Bingley as if she herself is not among the 'appallingly outrageous'. "At least, Lady Cilia appears to have had some tolerably good breeding and possesses some decorum not to look too ridiculously desperate. But the other two! They are utterly despicable! But even Lady Cilia is not to be taken lightly, because, though she might not go about in that abominably forward manner of the other two, she is more cunning. And as she is more subtle, it can be argued that she is more dangerous. She employs rather more underhand ways to try to insinuate herself into Mr

Darcy's good books. But do not worry, Louisa. I will not let her. I make absolutely sure that none of them shall be even a second alone with Mr Darcy."

So, I seem to have been right to place great hopes in those four ladies' vying with each other and acting as perfect foils for my master.

I next pass by another room. This one, I believe, is given to Mr Bingley, but Mr Hurst seems to be visiting him as I overhear Mr Hurst's voice from within talking to Mr Bingley.

"Bingley, have you heard the rumour about Darcy's having a lady's miniature concealed in his pocket very close to his heart?"

I prick up my ears. A rumour circulating concerning my master's miniature!? How can it be?

"Darcy!? Has a miniature of a lady concealed in his pocket!?" Mr Bingley gives out a cry of incredulity. "Are you in jest, Hurst!? Or are you foxed? Darcy would be the last man upon earth to have such a maudlin inclination!"

"Why should I jest about such a thing?" protests Mr Hurst. "Louisa has told me that the rumour states that some ladies are claiming that they have seen Darcy secretly take out a miniature from the breast pocket of his coat which naturally is the closest to his heart and look at it in a most caressing manner, and they also insist that the expression in Darcy's eyes when he did so was beyond all dispute that of a man deeply and desperately in love."

"If you believe in such a ludicrous rumour, you will believe in anything," says Mr Bingley in a dismissive tone. "You know what ladies are like. They have a tremendous power of imagination, and have this well-known tendency to make a tiny molehill into a mountain. Most likely, some lady saw Darcy take out a fob watch from his coat pocket and smile finding it was time he could decamp. And such an ordinary scene, in the lady's active imagination, must have turned into 'Darcy taking out a miniature of a lady and looking at it in ecstasy'."

"But you do agree, do you not," Mr Hurst persists, "that Darcy is not quite himself these days? He is absent-minded, and that is an understatement if there ever were one."

"If he seems absent-minded, it is much more likely that he is considering a chess move or absorbed in some deep philosophical contemplation. The thoughts of love or ladies are too paltry for Darcy. He will not waste his precious time on such prosaic matters."

"Prosaic matters, you say? But all thinkers, great philosophers and poets alike, have always copiously written about 'love' and 'ladies' at great length. There is nothing out of the ordinary if Darcy, too, indulges in such thoughts."

"Well, be that as it may, I still cannot imagine Darcy to be hankering after a lady insomuch that he will carry a miniature of the lady around! That picture sits wholly incongruously with his image."

"Oh, but we all know that 'love' can make a man, or indeed a woman to a greater degree, behave in a most uncharacteristic manner. That is a well known fact."

Mr Hurst, who is normally indolent, dim, and has no interest in anything other than sleeping, eating, and playing at cards, and whom I have never heard utter a single word remotely intelligent, is showing his entirely unknown insightful side, to my utter flabbergastation.

But can it really be true that my master has been so heedless as to let himself be seen taking the miniature of Miss Elizabeth out of his pocket? If it is, it certainly shows that my master indeed is not at all his usual self.

* * * * *

Today, I am visiting the Hursts' residence in Grosvenor Street with my master. Of course, I do not usually accompany my master to his friends' or acquaintances' residences, but the Hursts' is an exception.

While they dine, I am allowed to wait in the drawing room.

The Hursts' residence is a very large, fine house, might be even larger than my master's London residence. But I think it lacks the elegance and the exquisite taste my master's house oozes. The Hursts' house is showy, its richness is ostentatious, if not to say gaudy, whereas my master's has a reined-in grandeur.

Mr Hurst does not own a country estate, which is why Mrs Hurst pressed Mr Bingley so strongly to settle in one, so that she and her husband could have somewhere to visit when they are tired of staying in Town. Mr Hurst is far too indolent to be coerced into purchasing a country estate, on which he would have to expend so much of his energy to manage. It is a fact that no gentlemen have to toil away themselves to oversee their estates, as they delegate the task to their land agents, bailiffs, stewards and such. But nevertheless, judging from the great number of hours my master has to sacrifice in his study at both his London residence and Pemberley, working away and poring over all sorts of documents, letters and ledgers, gentlemen also, if they consider themselves to be conscientious landlords, seem to have a great deal to do.

The dinner seems to have finished, and Mrs Hurst and Miss Bingley have left the gentlemen with their port in the dining room and now have returned to the drawing room. I sit, or rather lie, in the shadowy corner and endeavour to make myself as invisible as possible. To my great comfort and satisfaction, the two ladies settle themselves upon the Chesterfield, facing away from me, and begin their conversation in whispering voices.

Upon the subject of the rumour concerning my master's miniature of Miss Elizabeth, Miss Bingley and Mrs Hurst now commence talking.

"Caroline," Mrs Hurst says to Miss Bingley, "I wish to talk to you about Mr Darcy's miniature, which Mrs Trevor claims she saw Mr Darcy gazing at. You said it was not your likeness after all as you once had thought it was, but you would not tell me whose it was."

"I do not wish to tell you, Louisa, because if it is known, it will reflect upon Mr Darcy badly as the lady in question is not someone whom a gentleman such as he should let occupy his heart."

"'Not someone whom a gentleman such as he should let occupy his heart'?" Mrs Hurst parrots. "Whoever can it be?"

Chapter 15

"Do not dwell upon it, as it is of no consequence," says Miss Bingley. "It is most unlikely that Mr Darcy will meet her again."

"'It is most unlikely that Mr Darcy will meet her again'?" Mrs Hurst parrots again. "Then, is she not of the *ton*? Is she not attending the London Season?"

"No, she is not and she never will, and Mr Darcy will do well to think of her no more. But Louisa, I have been thinking ... Should I not make use of this situation to establish my position as the foremost candidate for Mr Darcy's matrimonial prize?"

"Eh? How do you mean?" Mrs Hurst asks.

"I mean, if we could somehow make others believe, or at least suspect, that it is my likeness that the miniature bears, I shall be able to kill two birds with one stone. They will pay due respect to me and might keep their distance from Mr Darcy."

"But how do you plan to do it? You could not possibly tell them that you are the mystery lady of Mr Darcy's miniature in as many words yourself, could you?"

"No, of course not. That would be too indecorous! No, it will have to be much more subtle. And so, I have formed this idea. Could you, Louisa, possibly mention it to people in a, how should I phrase it, periphrastic fashion? Circumlocution is the best way to make people suspect things. If you are to be too direct, people will probably think it is just a fatuous, illusionary boast, and it will be a problem if it is known in the future that you have intentionally lied." Mrs Hurst here nods assent. "But, Louisa," Miss Bingley continues, "if you are to do it in a circumlocutory, rather vague manner, mark my words, they will begin to wonder what is hidden behind the words, and suspect all sorts of possibilities, and what is more important, we shall have no danger of being accused of having lied later."

"That is a capital idea, Caroline! I will wait for a good opportunity to begin the campaign, then," says Mrs Hurst, and here the gentlemen, too, return to the drawing room, and for the time being the conversation is laid aside.

Chapter 15

* * * * *

The scheme seemed to have been put into practice accordingly. This is how it came about as stated by Mrs Hurst.

At the ball held at Lord and Lady Weymouth's, a Mrs Cavendish – a matron of some forty summers with a couple of daughters whom she wishes to thrust firmly onto the path to matrimony this season – pulled Mrs Hurst aside and earnestly whispered into her ear, "My dear Mrs Hurst, have you heard the rumour circulating about a miniature of a lady that Mr Darcy carries close to his heart? Is there really a solid ground for such a tale? I believe your brother, Mr Bingley, is Mr Darcy's most intimate and trusted friend, am I not correct? Surely, if anyone is to know who Mr Darcy's lady is, your brother must be the one. Have you heard anything about it from your brother?"

"A thing of this nature is a highly sensitive affair," answered Mrs Hurst. "Nothing has been said, let alone settled as far as I know, and knowing Mr Darcy's disposition well, I very much fear that any irresponsible interference from outside or even inquisitiveness of others could only act as hindrance, if not deterrence for him, and we outsiders have to be very mindful of it. So, my lips are firmly sealed upon the subject." And Mrs Hurst left it at that, assuming a meaningful half smile upon her lips.

As Mrs Hurst and Miss Bingley had fully anticipated, this kind of talk only fuelled the interest of Mrs Cavendish, and she immediately went and repeated what Mrs Hurst had said with a little embellishment to her friends, who in their turn did the same, again with a few extra tit-bits, which procedure, as foreseen, was duly repeated a few more times.

And thus, that Miss Bingley might be the subject of my master's miniature now seems to be often talked of by the *ton*, but whether they really believe the verity of it or not is another matter altogether.

Well, I trust to god that no real harm will come from this scheme of these two conniving ladies. In light of what I know of how the *ton*'s mechanism works, as long as my master is duly mindful of not getting himself in a compromising position with the lady, or indeed with any lady, for that matter, all will be well.

* * * * *

Miss Bingley seems to be trying with all her might to be coy, happy and even flirtatious in my master's presence in a desperate bid to give credence to the rumour. But the *ton* seem to be becoming more disbelieving by the day, as my master's total lack of assiduity and warmth towards the lady who is supposed to be his heart's choice has been noted by all.

Can it really be possible, they seem to be questioning themselves, that a man, who is said to be so in love as to carry his love's miniature close to his heart and not to be able to part with it even for a second, should seem so uninterested in the lady and so utterly unaffected by her presence?

So as I thought, the sisters' scheme seems to have done no real harm to my master whatsoever.

* * * * *

The London Season is finally at an end, and my master has come out of it whole and hale to my great relief.

During this season, my master seems to have realized that Mr Bingley, who he thought had long since forgotten about Miss Bennet, still carries a torch for her, which is still as strongly aflame as it was last November, if not more strongly ablaze. And remembering Miss Elizabeth's strong censure against his meddling, he is very much perturbed. Maybe, he will decide to make a clean breast of it to Mr Bingley someday soon, and advise him to return to Hertfordshire.

* * * * *

We are to head for Derbyshire in a few days well in advance for the Glorious Twelfth. I heartily look forward to being able to serve my master in my full capacity as a gun dog.

Chapter 15

As well as the usual crowd, Mr Bingley, Miss Bingley, and the Hursts, my master, has invited a few other of his friends to make the party.

I will have to step up the level of my vigilance again at Pemberley. At busier times like during the London Season, when there are so many people around my master, Miss Bingley tends to be a little more subtle in her behaviour, no doubt, for fear of making herself look too ridiculous a figure. But such occasions of private country sojourn as these are the times when Miss Bingley becomes the most audacious in her pursuit of my master. Especially, as she has not succeeded in achieving her aim during the Season, she will be making every possible effort to weaken my master's defence.

I have to be well prepared.

Chapter 15

Chapter 16

In which my master goes to Pemberley, where he has an unexpected, happy re-encounter, which, alas, turns out not so happy later

My master, as he wishes to attend to some outstanding estate business before the guests arrive tomorrow, has left his sister and his friends at the Eagle in Leicester to stay another night, and is now continuing the journey to Pemberley with only Mr Trent and me accompanying him.

I am having this hunch that something is imminent. An acute feeling almost like euphoria is permeating my body. Whatever can it be?

* * * * *

The coach is now just turning into the sweep in front of the carriage house at the rear of the Pemberley House.

An odd feeling of urgency in me steadily grew as we neared Pemberley, and has been getting stronger and surer by the second. I feel in my bones that something momentous awaits us, and am now too impatient to wait till the carriage comes to a halt.

I jump precipitately out of the open carriage window.

"Watch out, Julius Caesar! Damn! What has got into you! That was too dangerous! You impatient rascal!" I hear my master's unusually panicked voice. "Stop the carriage!"

I run and run, but look back momentarily to see my master himself jumping out of the coach even before it rocks to a halt and without waiting for the footman to tug open the door. I then hear my master, too, start running after me.

I run and run, never minding my master calling after me to stop. I run like a mad dog, impelled and driven by this unaccountable impulse to hurry with all my might as if something were hauling and tugging me forward. My master, still panicked and perturbed by my precipitancy, rushes after me, still calling my name.

Oh, my unerring, ever dependable intuition! Yes, the hunch I had that something was imminent was absolutely accurate! I know my master has as yet no notion whatsoever, but, oh, my superior olfactories perceive, definitely sense Miss Elizabeth's presence! Yes! Yes! I can positively smell her! Improbable as it may be, she must be here at Pemberley!

Conscious of my tail wagging like mad, I rush around the corner towards where my acute sense tells me Miss Elizabeth is at the moment, while my master calls after me from far behind, bidding me not to rush so. How can I not rush when I anticipate this momentous encounter! I wonder what my master's reaction will be when he sees his beloved Miss Elizabeth. I place any odds that my master's heart will be set aflutter like a delicate bird's wings.

There she is, as large as life and twice as enchanting! She is poised there, her head turned doubtless to look behind to see who the proponent of the noisy barks is. I sense the very moment she realizes that it is I, Julius Caesar, who am running up to her. She becomes manifestly flustered, when her mind, as I suspect, logically follows that I am here, wherefore, my master, too, must be.

Having thus realized that I am here, Miss Elizabeth timorously raises her eyes in expectation, no doubt, of seeing my master behind me. My acute auditory sense detects her suddenly quickened heartbeat. Is it an auspicious sign? Yes, I believe it is! The simple fact alone that Miss Elizabeth is here visiting Pemberley must surely suggest that the intense aversion she formerly felt towards my master has materially diminished. Much as I wish to take credit for having made her see sense by showing her my master's miniature of her and that letter from Mr Wickham to my master, I must acknowledge that my master's letter to her had already made her regard my master in a little more kindly way before I showed her those items.

Here is my master! He has just come round the corner while chiding me for my rash antics, and shows his noble self though rather a-panting from his exertion. Then, noticing a lady standing, and in whom immediately recognizing Miss Elizabeth, my master abruptly halts in his tracks and his eyes open wide as if they were about to bulge out of their sockets.

How truly astounding! I have never ever seen my master come anywhere near to blushing before, nor have I ever seen him even faintly flustered. But now, the deep red hue has spread over his handsome visage, as the maidenly pink also dyes Miss Elizabeth's blossoming cheeks at the same time, and my master is stuttering and floundering with words, making deuced clumsy attempts at making conversation. And moreover, he is in such confusion that he has not even noticed that Miss Elizabeth has company!

Oh, dear God, no! My master is so damned flustered that he has given up his futile efforts at engaging in small talk, bows to Miss Elizabeth, turns on his heels and decamps!

But I know all too well that my master will wish to go after Miss Elizabeth the moment he comes out of his dazed state and regains his composure. So, I rush after my master, so that I can be of help when the time comes to track Miss Elizabeth expeditiously by dint of my superior sense of smell.

Reaching his bedchamber, he all but drops himself into his chair and sits there gazing into space for a deuced long while, as I impatiently grind my teeth, hoping my master will come out of this state of

Chapter 16

stupefaction before it is too late.

My master, then, rises, and I jump up expectantly, assuming that he is now ready to go, but contrary to my expectation, he starts pacing the length of the room distractedly, muttering some incoherent words which I presume are something in the line of, "Good God! I must be hallucinating! Is Miss Elizabeth really here? It can't be! Or can it? Am I drunk? But I haven't touched any liquor!"

He paces to and fro for another deuced long time, and I grind my teeth yet again.

But at last, thanks be to god, like a man suddenly awoken from a dream, my master stops dead and peers around the room as if he had woken to find himself in a weird place. He slaps his own face a few times to whip himself out of his stupor. And as the full import of the present situation settles over him, he berates himself for his lack of composure, which might result in his losing the god-given opportunity of setting the past to rights.

He rushes out of his chamber in a great hustle and bustle no doubt to go on his way in search of Miss Elizabeth. With alacrity, I rush out, too, and follow him.

Emerging from the house, my master suddenly halts and looks right and left in great agitation apparently realizing he has not a clue how to ascertain which route Miss Elizabeth has taken. This is the time I was waiting for, the time for my glory! I will know exactly which way Miss Elizabeth has gone! I raise my nose and sniff the air. Yes! Yes!

Looking up at my master, I bark thrice sharply and succinctly, willing him to understand my meaning, as it is an unstated code which I habitually employ when I wish him to follow me during hunts, and then dash forward hot on Miss Elizabeth's trail.

I now and then look back to make sure that my master is following.

While my master was shilly-shallying up in his bedchamber, Miss Elizabeth, who must be being shown around the grounds, seems to have gone quite a long way, and it is taking quite a while to catch up with her.

But here she is at last! I espy the dainty figure of Miss Elizabeth strolling with her companions guided by Mr Jones, the head gardener, and I know that my master, too, has caught sight of her as I sense the tell-tale chemical oozing out of his person ...

I dearly hope that, instead of being thrown into a dithering state again as he was earlier, my master will now be able to use this opportunity to his fullest advantage and try and ascertain that Miss Elizabeth should see the real him and amend her former impression of him.

I think fast. To allow both Miss Elizabeth and my master ample time to ready themselves, and also to prepare the way for them to an easy beginning, I run up to Miss Elizabeth so that she can greet me and pet me. She lowers herself to do so, and laughingly, though the laugh is a little tremulous, pats my head and hugs my body, muttering greetings and terms of endearment, while my master approaches, with rather an awkward gait as if he cannot quite decide which leg should coordinate with which arm.

Upon my master's approach, Miss Elizabeth rises and with a somewhat wavery smile and a quivering voice remarks, “Julius Caesar is full of spirit as always.”

“Yes, he is tremendously excited to see you,” says my master in reply. He ought to add here, “And so am I.” But of course, as he is endowed with no such skill of pleasantry, all he can do is to add, “You are a great favourite of his.” He should also add, “And mine, too,” here, if he had any flair for flirting. But I am perfectly aware that is much too much to ask for. I might as well cry for the moon as wish my master suddenly to become an adept in love.

Thus the ice broken and the passage made smoother, I hope it will be easier for them to proceed with the confirmation of their happy reacquaintance.

My master seems to have gained enough presence of mind to spare a thought for Miss Elizabeth's companions and asks her to introduce them to him, which Miss Elizabeth accordingly does and my master learns that these people are Miss Elizabeth's uncle and aunt.

Chapter 16

Miss Elizabeth's mildly amused face here makes me a little puzzled. Then, I recall Dixon's account of my master's disastrous proposal of marriage back in April, in which my master exasperated Miss Elizabeth by most unwisely dwelling upon her inferior connections. My master is indeed damned fortunate that Miss Elizabeth, rather than to be angered anew by the recollection, seems to find it amusing instead that my master is now thus eagerly seeking to be introduced to the very people whom he labelled as unworthy relatives back then.

I examine Miss Elizabeth's countenance closely, and am happy to conclude that her sentiments towards my master now are not at all what they were then. The somewhat defiant, stern lights which I would so often see dart across her eyes formerly when she was with my master are now replaced by far tenderer expressions, and if I cannot be so bold as to say with firm conviction that they are those of love, I dare say that I can be bold enough to say that they may well be in time.

They all start walking together.

First, my master walks with Miss Elizabeth's uncle, Mr Gardiner, and Miss Elizabeth with her aunt, Mrs Gardiner. But after sometime, they exchange partners, and by happy arrangement Miss Elizabeth becomes my master's walking parter.

Neither of them look entirely comfortable, but my master is faring far better than I would ever have imagined him capable, and when mentioning the party of people expected to arrive tomorrow, has even bolstered up enough courage to ask Miss Elizabeth to allow him to introduce his sister to her. Miss Elizabeth thanks him and says she would indeed be very happy and honoured to know his sister, and I am sure she really means it and feels genuinely gratified.

My master's face becomes infused with such joy that I almost feel like crying. But of course, dogs do not cry like humans do. Though we do shed tears now and then, ours are not caused by emotions. So, when I say I feel like crying, I am only talking figuratively. I just feel as if I were a father who is looking over his son's progress with deep love and concern. And if I were, I would surely pat my master's shoulder and say to him, "Well done, son!"

I feel quite proud to have been the direct means of facilitating their reunion thus. Had my hunch not assisted me and made me run and run in that wise when we arrived at Pemberley, Miss Elizabeth would have left that spot before we arrived and my master would have missed the opportunity entirely.

* * * * *

Things, I am fully persuaded, virtually never proceed as smoothly as one would expect. My master had two glorious days, and would have expected those to continue.

Firstly, he took his beloved sister to meet his beloved Miss Elizabeth and saw them derive great happiness from getting acquainted with each other. Secondly, he felt greatly relieved to see Miss Elizabeth meet Mr Bingley again with apparently good spirit, which showed that she did not bear any grudge against Mr Bingley for forsaking her sister. Thirdly, he enjoyed fishing with Miss Elizabeth's uncle, Mr Gardiner. Fourthly, he had the joy of having Miss Elizabeth at Pemberley again when she came to return Miss Darcy's visit, although Miss Bingley's all familiar jealous and acrimonious attitude towards Miss Elizabeth upon the occasion was a blot on his otherwise supreme happiness. And last but not least, he was made exceedingly happy to be convinced that Miss Elizabeth's sentiments towards him had much improved.

* * * * *

So, this morning, my master, whose fond heart could hardly wait to see Miss Elizabeth again, eagerly presented himself at the inn where Miss Elizabeth and her uncle and aunt were staying, anticipating an enchanting time which he would spend with Miss Elizabeth.

But what awaited my master was not the enchanting encounter of his anticipation, but Miss Elizabeth in despair and most disturbing news from her home, Longbourn – that her youngest sister, Miss

Lydia, had fallen under the evil spell of Mr Wickham and had eloped with him. It seemed that the militia had moved to Brighton from Meryton, and Miss Lydia, invited by the wife of the colonel, had followed them thither. There being no one to keep her under strict and constant surveillance, the rather fast, unthinking girl must have been easy prey for a seasoned libertine of Mr Wickham's calibre.

My master's face turned as white as a sheet upon hearing the news.

Miss Elizabeth was to leave for home at the earliest expediency. She, fearing the worst – Miss Lydia's ruin and as a result, the total disgrace of the whole family – was in a fit of tears, and lamented that nothing could be done.

I knew that the distressing memory of his own sister's near ruin by the hand of the same villain rushed back to my master's mind. Miss Darcy had been fortunate enough to be saved from utter ruin by her brother's opportune arrival. But what about Miss Lydia?

I sensed my master's mind working rapidly then and there forming a plan – a plan to search out the fugitives' retreat himself. Of course, my master is a far more likely person than any other to be able to track the fugitives down because of his greater knowledge of Mr Wickham's history and connections.

And my master bade Miss Elizabeth farewell with great pain on parting.

* * * * *

Now my master is in his bedchamber all set to start for London at the crack of dawn tomorrow morning.

As it is often the method of consoling himself when he is in distress, he sits holding me tight, his face half buried in the fur of the back of my neck.

"Ah, Julius Caesar," says my master with his voice muffled by my fur, "the image of Miss Elizabeth's lovely face tormented and streaked with tears of anguish would not leave me! How I wished to hold her in my arms and soothe her! Even wiping her hot tears from her cheeks with my own lips!"

Chapter 16

Of course, if he knew the extent of my understanding, he would never have uttered such embarrassingly maudlin words.

"Oh," he ejaculates, "how I wished I could give her comforting words! How I wished to promise her that everything would be all right, to tell her that I would do everything in my power to find her sister and bring her back to the safe bosom of her family. But how could I? I have no guarantee. It would have been cruel to raise vain hopes in Miss Elizabeth's heart without the surest of confidence. Oh, but should I have done so? Should I have gathered her in my arms and told her what I was going to do? Should I have given her some respite from anguish and uncertainty however momentary?"

Thus, my master continues to mutter into the back of my neck.

Chapter 16

Chapter 17

In which my master travels to London to track down the fugitives

This morning, my master rose with the sun, and he and I, and naturally, my master's gentleman's gentleman, the indispensable Mr Trent, too, are now already upon the road for the hundred and fifty mile journey to the capital.

In my master's severe, ponderous profile as he gazes out of the window of the carriage at the flying scene outside, I see his determination, his firm resolve not to rest until he has discovered the fugitives' whereabouts.

* * * * *

We have just arrived in Town after nearly, twenty hours of hard run without many substantial halts at the inns, and the coach is now trundling along the last stretch to my master's townhouse.

Judging from his face and the way he carries himself, Mr Trent is distinctly the worse for wear after the long and vigorous journey. My master, the culprit, who bade his coachmen hurry the horses to the fullest limit, being too impatient to reach London to allow any dilly-dallying upon the road, seems now to be feeling a little penitent for having made Mr Trent, who is in no wise a young man any longer, suffer thus.

"Trent, I am very sorry not to have considered your comfort more," says my master to Mr Trent.

"It is I, sir, who have to apologise for being such a useless traveller, and for having made you worry about me unnecessarily," says Mr Trent, with a little shaky voice, "but I thank you for your kind words and concern. I know perfectly well, sir, that there must be a reason of paramount importance for your great haste, and I beg of you not to worry about me. I am perfectly all right, sir."

My master, who is still feeling guilty, bids Mr Trent retire to his room immediately and rest.

* * * * *

My master has decided that the only possible thread which could lead to finding Mr Wickham's place of retreat would be Mrs Younge, Miss Darcy's former governess, who infamously exploited her trusted position and lent a hand to Mr Wickham's satanic attempt upon Miss Darcy in July of last year.

So, come tomorrow morning, the first thing my master will do will be to visit his man of business, Mr Seymour, who, according to my master, is a man of exceptional ability, a lawyer cum some sort of private investigator, who has many a pertinent piece of information about all the past and the present employees for the Darcy household.

My master believes that Mr Seymour will be able to provide him with the address of Mrs Younge's present dwelling.

* * * * *

My master's reliance upon his man of business has not been misplaced as my master has been duly given the directions to the abode of Mrs Younge, the above mentioned former employee of dubious character.

Chapter 17

My master knocks thrice sharply rat-tat-tat with his walking stick on the door of the house in Edward Street, which is where Mrs Younge is supposed to be now living. Mrs Younge, according to Mr Seymour, runs a boarding house here.

A maid of a rather slatternly appearance opens the door and begs to know my master's business.

"Is this the abode of the matron by the name of Mrs Younge?" asks my master.

"Y...yes, s...sir," stutters the maid, looking not a little daunted by my master's severe voice with no inflection.

"Go and tell your mistress that Mr Darcy of Pemberley is here," intones my master.

"Y...yes, yes, s...sir, at once!" the maid stutters again, drops a small curtsy, and scuttles off down the corridor and disappears through the door at the far end of it. My acute auditory sense detects low voices of two females.

The maid after some moments returns with quick hurried steps, and even more awkwardly than formerly stammers out with an awfully harried face, "I...I am s...sorry, s...sir, I m...must have been m...mistaken. M..my m...mistress does not seem to be h...h...home."

It stands out a mile that she is being mendacious, obviously bidden by her mistress.

My master brushes the maid aside and without heeding the maid's flustered remonstrations, strides towards the door, which he flings open, and goes in. Of course, I follow suit.

And there stands Mrs Younge, with a shocked expression, with her palm pressed to her chest.

"Why, Mr Darcy! This is trespassing! I will have you know!" she cries out, and opens and shuts her mouth like a fish deficient in oxygen.

"So, what? Are you going to send for a Bow Street runner? Go ahead if you dare," my master says in an frightfully icy monotone icier than even the real ice could ever aspire to be, which makes Mrs Younge clamp her mouth shut.

"I am looking for someone of your close acquaintance, who has absconded with a girl. I am sure you know whom I am referring to," says my master, eyeing Mrs Young ever so frostily.

"You are mistaken," says Mrs Younge defensively. "I have not the faintest idea of whom your are talking."

"It is pointless to deny it, Mrs Younge," drawls my master. "But if you insist you do not know, I shall be kind enough to let you know. I am talking of Wickham, and of course, you know where his hideout is."

"How should I know? I have not seen him for more than a year," returns Mrs Younge in a guarded but insolent voice.

"Come now, Mrs Younge, be more reasonable," says my master casually, but with deathly ruthlessness almost tangible underneath. "You know very well such prevarication will not work. Wickham has no other close acquaintance in Town. Who else is there whom he could turn to that has enough knowledge of the capital and is depraved enough to give succour to such goings-on?"

* * * * *

Mrs Younge has been stubbornly maintaining her claim that she knows nothing of Mr Wickham's whereabouts, but has now finally come as far as to admit that he did indeed come to her for help when he arrived in London, but she still refuses to reveal where he is.

* * * * *

My master has achieved his objective. The whereabouts of Mr Wickham and Miss Lydia have at last been discovered.

I hate to be boastful, but I have played a crucial role in it.

Mrs Younge, obviously intent upon seeking as big a recompense as she could get from my master, was obdurate enough not to give in too quickly, and come the evening of the second day, which was yesterday, she had still not bowed to the pressure that my master placed her under.

My master decided to raise the sum of money to offer as a bribe to such a level as to make it absolutely impossible for Mrs Younge to resist. She would extort from my master hundreds and hundreds of guineas. I heartily detested the idea of such an immoral, avaricious, abhorrent woman getting the better of my noble master, but knew that it could not be helped.

So, this morning, my master again knocked on her door. A faithful dog that I was, I was of course at his side.

The same maid answered and told my master that her mistress was abroad at the time but she would be back in half an hour or thereabouts. My master said he would wait, and we were ushered into a parlour which we had not set foot in before.

The moment I entered the parlour, however, I detected a vaguely familiar smell, which at once nagged and niggled my mind. After cogitating hard for a while, wondering and trying to locate whose scent it was, I suddenly realized that it was that of Mr Wickham's! I had smelt him but twice up till then, once when my master had confronted him in Ramsgate in the summer of last year, having discovered Mr Wickham's villainous scheme to elope with Miss Darcy, and once a few months later in November, when my master had happened across Mr Wickham in the street of Meryton, and I, too, had been accompanying him. But twice was more than sufficient. I pride in my very superior sense of smell, as I might have often mentioned.

There was absolutely no room for doubt that Mr Wickham had been there in the parlour not long since, and as I had detected no trace of Mr Wickham's smell along the corridor, Mr Wickham must have come and gone by way of some other route, which only left the French windows.

I barked thrice as the frequently practised code to mean that I wished my master to follow me, which I think I have mentioned once before. I also grabbed hold of the hem of my master's coat with my mouth and gave him a little tug to make it doubly sure he understood, though I was duly heedful not to damage his coat of superfine.

Understanding my meaning, my master told the maid that he had decided not to wait for her mistress after all. Upon that cue, I dashed out of the French window, and followed Mr Wickham's trail, my master hot on my heels.

As I said, my sense of smell is very superior, and as long as the trail does not disappear into a waterway, I seldom fail to follow a scent however faint its trail is.

Mr Wickham's trail was rather faint, but not so faint as to pose serious difficulties for me. It was, however, deuced desultory, now going this way, and now turning that way, with no definite direction, absolutely typical of that irresponsible, degenerate, utterly godless villain of a man.

The first notable place that my nose led me to was an establishment looking rather seedy from outside, a tell-tale sign of three golden balls denoting that the premises was a pawnbroker's.

Yes, if Mr Wickham had not already sold all the finest of the gowns and jewels which Miss Lydia had brought from Longbourn to Brighton, then from Brighton to London, I would eat my hat, I said to myself. Of course, I was talking only metaphorically, as I am a dog and I do not wear a hat, though I have on occasions seen some of my fellow canines looking devilish uncomfortable and, might I say, not a little silly, wearing hats hoisted on them by their masters or mistresses.

Mr Wickham's trail continued after leaving the pawnshop with numerous more deviations.

The next place of note after the pawnbroker's was what could only be described as an establishment belonging to the dubious province of *demi-monde*.

“He cannot refrain from visiting these places of ill-repute even while thus in hiding having eloped with an innocent girl!” my master said with a huge sigh, seeming far too disgusted even to feel angry. “I have not expected this even from Wickham!”

I could very easily have expected it from Mr Wickham, I thought.

So, had he spent the money from the pawnbroker's on dallying with prostitutes? I felt deep, deep pity for Miss Lydia. Granted that Miss

Lydia, as I remember, was rather a silly light-weight of a girl always chasing after officers, she is still a mere child, only fifteen or sixteen, and does not deserve such a man.

Mr Wickham's trail continued after that in a manner of eastwards.

"I am afraid of having a guess at what Wickham's next port of call was," my master groaned. "I fear it might have been a gaming den."

But to my master's great relief, Mr Wickham did not seem to have visited any of those, at least on that occasion in any event, and in due course, my nose led us to a shabby house in a shabby street in the shabby district of the Strand.

* * * * *

My nose never errs. My master has found, upon inquiry, that in the garret of this house, Mr Wickham did indeed find accommodation with the aid of Mrs Younge, and he and Miss Lydia have been lodging here for these ten days ever since they arrived in London.

I feel heartily gratified to have thus been the means of leading my master to Mr Wickham and Miss Lydia, but equally importantly, I am exceedingly chuffed to have been able to thwart Mrs Younge's plan of extorting money from my beloved master. I cannot help a wide grin spreading when I imagine how that despicable, grabbing, unprincipled woman will be gnashing her teeth when she realizes that she has missed her great chance of receiving her reward!

* * * * *

My master is now poised in front of the garret room before knocking the door, whence a woman's somewhat petulant voice is heard.

"You are a great miser of a man, Wickham!" says the voice. "Why can you not take me out? Just to a theatre or for shopping. And ... oh, yes, Gunter's Tea Shop! I have read about the shop in magazines so many times! We must taste Gunter's ices when we are in London! That, I dare say, is an absolute must!"

"You know very well, Lydia, you cannot go out in case you are seen," says the voice of Mr Wickham. "And where do you suppose I can acquire money to indulge ourselves in such frivolous activities?"

He has money enough to fritter away upon a bit of muslin, I snort.

"I do not see why I should not be allowed to go out when you go out as often as the whim takes you. And in any event, who would recognize me in Town? I have no acquaintances here. At least you could take me out just to sight-see, which would not cost you a penny! There! How reasonable I am!"

"Have you forgotten that you have an uncle and an aunt here? And most likely your father would have come up to Town by now in search of his beloved daughter."

"Well, if I am seen, I am seen. What is there so disastrous in that?"

"If you are discovered, you will have to be separated from me and go home. If you do not mind that, go ahead."

"Why should I be separated from you? I shall only have to say No and they will not be able to do anything about it! Because we are going to be married, are we not, you and I?"

"Yes, yes, yes, when the time comes. But not yet," says Mr Wickham, in a most careless, off-handed fashion, more in the spirit of 'when hell freezes over'.

"Why can we not get married immediately? What is there to prevent us?" protests Miss Lydia.

"It costs a lot of money to marry, much more than an ignorant chit like you could ever have any idea, and takes a lot of preparations, too. It will be a long, long time yet before we can even begin to think of marriage."

Is marriage really on his agenda? Pigs might fly.

My master raises his hand and knocks on the door several times really loudly in hurried succession. The voices inside cease and a few moments later, the doorknob turns.

"Yes, yes, yes, do not be so impatient! What do you want?" Mr Wickham shouts, opening the door with one hand, the other raking through his hair irritatedly.

There is a momentary silence during which the utterly flabbergasted man grapples with his own senses and realizes that it is really Mr Darcy as large as life who he sees standing in front of him.

"M ... Mr Darcy!?" he splatters out. "Why are you here!?"

"To whip you within an inch of your life and make you into a man of a little more decency and discipline. Why else!?" says my master.

Miss Lydia, who obviously is very curious, sneaks up behind Mr Wickham, and peeks through the gap between the said gentleman and the door frame.

"Good Lord! It is really Mr Darcy!" she cries out. "Why, Wickham! Do not tell me we have been discovered! But surely, Mr Darcy, you do not really mean to whip my dear Wickham within an inch of his life, do you!?"

Though the situation is hardly a laughing matter, my master seems unable to help a wry smile at such an ultimately nincompoopish address.

"No, Miss Lydia, it is a mere figure of speech. I have no intention of really whipping Wickham. You may rest assured," says my master ... a trifle patronisingly as if he were talking to a child ... or a nincompoop.

"Wickham, first of all, I ought to have a word with you. Lead the way to somewhere we can talk privately," commands my master.

Mr Wickham nods uncertainly as if he would much rather not, but does as he is bidden, and telling Miss Lydia to wait in the room, there's a good girl, shows my master to a parlour on the ground floor.

It must be the premier reception room of the house, but is a mangy room looking rather poverty-stricken, with a few forlorn threadbare chairs carelessly scattered about in it. I did not look into the garret room, but if the reception room is in this wise, it does not take much power of imagination to picture the state of the bedrooms.

Looking about the room with some expression of disgust, my master turns to Mr Wickham.

"To suffer Miss Lydia, a lady genteelly brought up in a decent environment, if not in the height of luxury, to live in such a squalid place," says my master severely, "have you no sense of courtesy, consideration or responsibility which a man should owe to a lady,

Wickham?"

"It is not my fault," says Mr Wickham. "It was not as if I asked Lydia to come. In truth, it was the reverse. I forbade her to come, but she would not listen and insisted upon accompanying me. I am the true victim in this."

"Do not try to lay the blame at another's door! Should it ever have been true that Miss Lydia insisted that you bring her with you totally against your intention, you could still have easily prevented her from taking such a path if you had been so minded. But I do not believe such was the case. You wantonly bowed to your baser instinct, and must have coaxed and cajoled an innocent girl into elopement and down the path to her utter ruin, dangling a false promise of marriage."

"But I have my heart set upon finding an heiress to marry," says Mr Wickham. "Why would I coax a girl with no prospect of bringing me any sizeable dowry to elope with me and jeopardise that possibility!?"

"Very easily. A lady's innocence is nothing to you. It is there to be trampled upon and only to be fodder to your unprincipled ego and sexual appetite."

Mr Wickham merely clams his mouth, no doubt, unable to deny it.

"That aside, what was it that impelled you to abscond, though I can easily conjecture," says my master. "Was it because of your gambling debts yet again? Did Brighton, too, become too hot to hold you?"

Mr Wickham remains obdurately silent, which betrays that my master's guess has hit the bull's eye.

"So, you cowardly decamped," continues my master, "and to make the flight more amenable and a little more fun, you chose to involve an innocent girl."

"Please stop repeating 'innocent girl', 'innocent girl'," protests Mr Wickham. "What is there so innocent about that girl? She was flirting and dallying with every man in an officer's uniform and playing a coquette from the very moment she arrived in Brighton! And in any event, what innocent girl would happily elope with a man with a mere lifting of a finger from the man?"

Chapter 17

"Hasn't the thought ever enter your mind that Miss Lydia might have agreed to elope with you because she is innocent, young and trusting, albeit unthinking?" says my master with a voice dark and threatening.

I very much suspect that the image of his own sister in July of last year, innocent, young and trusting, nearly being persuaded into eloping by this same silver-tongued villain has come back to pain my master anew.

The similar thought to mine may have occurred to Mr Wickham, as he hurriedly says,

"I did not mean that Miss Darcy was not innocent because she agreed to elope with me, as in her case ..."

"How dare you mention my sister!" my master snarls. "For you to utter her name is defilement itself!"

And I totally agree with my master. A man such as Mr Wickham does not deserve even to mention Miss Darcy, who is all that is good and saintly.

"But now, other than anything else, we should be thinking of Miss Lydia," says my master. "I will talk to her. Judging from what I overheard her saying, it is evident that Miss Lydia believes that your intentions are honourable, and means to marry you. As a responsible member of society, however, I feel it is my duty to try to dissuade her from such a path. Of course it is strictly for her sake, never for yours, Wickham. But if I find her absolutely immutable, then, you shall marry her. I do not know, and do not even wish to know, Wickham, how many young innocent ladies you might have trifled with and ruined with impunity so far, but consider this to be the last time you shall do so."

"Neither my affairs nor Lydia's, Mr Darcy, if I may remind you, have anything whatever to do with you," says Mr Wickham, putting on a bold front.

"You are mistaken!" says my master. "This is a business which no one with any decency, sense of responsibility and conscience should stand by and let pass, and I for one certainly will not."

Chapter 17

Mr Wickham looks as if he wishes to say something in retort again, but seems to think twice and maintains a sullen silence.

"By the by," my master says, levelling a steady gaze at Mr Wickham, "what is the sum of your debt?"

Mr Wickham raises his head expectantly, a sanguine light replaces the sullen expression in his eyes.

"Em ..." he hesitates. The sum must be enormous. "I am not sure exactly, but ... it might be as much as a thousand pounds."

A thousand pounds!? Hell and damnation! And if my grasp of human nature, especially of such as Mr Wickham's ilk, this figure is an underestimate and the actual sum is likely to be infinitely larger. Mr Wickham at least seems to have the decency to look ashamed.

But my master does not even bat an eyelid.

"Go and fetch Miss Lydia," my master bids Mr Wickham, "and after that, wait in your room like a good man. A word of advice. Do not even think of escaping. Think carefully. I always gave you a helping hand when you were in the same kind of trouble and in need of money. I promised myself never to do so again, but I will break that promise for Miss Lydia's sake one more time. I will help you defray your debts if you do as I bid and behave yourself. I may even consider doing more than that."

* * * * *

My master is now having a word with Miss Lydia.

While he is doing so in the parlour downstairs, Mr Wickham, as was bidden, waits in the garret room, outside which I keep a close vigil lest he should try to escape. Surprisingly, he remains in the room docilely.

Once he opened the door, though I do not know for what purpose, but I growled menacingly baring my teeth, pretending to be a fierce bruiser of a fighting dog that I am not. I am an English Setter, a tender-hearted dog. My friendliness, amiableness and even-temper are legendary, and looking fearsome is not my forte. I had no idea whether I was being convincingly intimidating or not. I rather suspect that, instead of looking fierce, I looked more like a mad dog 'grinning like a Cheshire cat' as John Wolcot once wrote in one of his poems. But maybe, my acting was excellent, as Mr Wickham upon seeing me immediately closed the door. Of course, it may well have been that he had no intention of leaving the room in the first place. Nonetheless, I should like to think that my growling did the business and I was of great service to my master.

Well ... it is, I admit, most likely that Mr Wickham has weighed the pros and cons of the situation and has decided that the specious prospect of the immediate release from the worry of the debts is far more attractive than the rather uncertain prospect of finding an heiress.

* * * * *

My master hoped that Miss Lydia would listen to his word of reason and see that marrying Wickham would be a deuced cork-brained idea and would never bring her happiness. But she was unshakable in her resolve to become his bride. She would not even lend half an ear to my master's plea to agree to be returned to her family.

"Why, Mr Darcy! You are such a pessimist! Do not be such a spoil-sport! You need not worry on my account as I mean to be unutterably happy with Wickham! He is such a dear, so handsome and so dashing! How green with envy my friends and my sisters will be! Oh, can you imagine how proud I shall be when I parade him in front of them! I cannot wait to see their faces! Indeed I cannot!" thus Miss Lydia rattled on with clamorous glee, and the only path for my master to pursue to remedy the evil done was to try and bring Miss Lydia's wish to fruition.

* * * * *

The business has been thoroughly discussed between my master and Mr Wickkam and has at last been settled. Miss Lydia is to marry Mr Wickham.

The sum of Mr Wickham's debts has proven to surpass even my

wildest guess. It amounts to only a few pennies short of a mighty two thousand pounds! A kind of sum which a man of Mr Wickham's low position and meagre potential could never ever find the means to pay back, that is, unless he went and held up a multitude of carriages upon the king's highways.

No wonder he is so willing to do as he is bidden by my master.

* * * * *

"You know, Julius Caesar," my master mutters to me and hugs me tight in his habitual manner, burying his face in my fur, which as per usual tickles me a little, "I wish to do everything there is to do for Miss Elizabeth on my own – arrange for Wickham and her sister's wedding, defray his debts, secure his future profession and set the couple's new life rolling. Because I want to be the one, the only one to serve Miss Elizabeth, to be instrumental in returning her life to its former tranquillity and to bring a smile back to her dear face. I will not let anyone else share that honour, be it her father, uncle or friends."

I just sit there docilely, quietly panting and slowly wagging my tail. The soft regular sound of my tail thumping the floor seems always to have a very calming effect upon my master.

"I shall have to let the Gardiners know," my master continues to mumble, "of the discovery of the elopers and my plans regarding their future. I know the Gardiners will not be easily persuaded and will insist that they cannot possibly let me bear all the burden. But, Julius Caesar, I shall have some good excuses at the ready, which in fact are no more than the truth. I will tell them that I hold myself wholly accountable for this calamity, as I, who was the only one in the position of knowing Wickham's evil propensity, should have imparted that knowledge to everybody. When they hear how deeply I regret not having done so, I am certain the Gardiners will understand and let me have my way."

* * * * *

Chapter 17

My master is now closeted with Mr and Mrs Gardiner in the drawing room of their house in Cheapside, discussing and re-discussing Mr Wickham and Miss Lydia's marriage and their future.

Mrs Gardiner shed the tears of gratitude when she heard that the fugitives had been found and that Wickham had consented to marry Miss Lydia.

My master insists everything be done by himself. But as my master predicted, the Gardiners will not hear of it. My master plays down the size of Mr Wickham's debts, hoping they will acquiesce. But still, the Gardiners insist they cannot possibly let my master shoulder all the burden. Whereupon my master gives them those plausible reasons he prepared why he deems himself the only one accountable, and my master's persistence carries the day in the end.

I have this sneaking suspicion, though, that the Gardiners, Mrs Gardiner in particular, with her keenly attuned female sense of perception, have fathomed the depth of my master's feelings towards Miss Elizabeth, and have divined where the true reason lies for my master's insistence to do everything himself.

Well, I suppose it would not have needed a stroke of genius for them to guess how smitten my master is by their niece. After all, he was all aflutter and even blushed deeply like a fair maiden, and stuttered and fumbled with words terribly like a veritable dullard, when he saw Miss Elizabeth at Pemberley.

If that had not been a sign that a man was madly in love, what would have?

* * * * *

This morning a marriage between Mr George Wickham and Miss Lydia Bennet was finally sanctified by God, and Miss Lydia became Mrs Wickham accordingly.

They have left for the north, for Newcastle to be precise, where they are to start a new life together. By dint of my master's contrivance and backing, Mr Wickham has acquired the ensigncy in the regular regiment stationed in that northern town. If I am honest, I am hoping that the general of the regiment will give Mr Wickham a good and proper thrashing.

Though he is hardly a man given to optimism, my master is nonetheless entertaining the vain hope that this can be the making of Mr Wickham and he will turn a new leaf.

In my humble opinion, it will indeed be a cold day in hell when that happens.

* * * * *

My master is now at the Gardiners' residence, having been invited to have dinner with them. The Gardiners kindly asked my master to bring me along with him, and I am now in their parlour, playing with their children while the adults dine.

The children are truly adorable. They are utterly different from many unruly ragamuffins I have encountered who would tug my tail and pull my ears hooping like barbarians, or many hoity-toity young masters and young ladies at the other end of the spectrum, who would look at me coldly as if I were something unworthy of their notice and too dirty to touch, or many a child who would back away from me scared, as if I were some savage ruffian dog prone to attacking people. The Gardiners' children are just the kind of children I most adore – well behaved, but without being boringly prim and proper, and with precisely the right level of mischief in them.

The adults have finished dinner and my master has now come into the room with the Gardiners.

My master, contrary to his outward impression of being rather a reserved, aloof man, has in fact an unexpected knack of becoming a great favourite of children. When he is with children, laughter lines appear beside the corners of his eyes and his usual rather unapproachable image instantly disappears and it seems as if a warm and friendly aura breathes through his person.

And this occasion is no exception. My master becomes at once a great favourite of the children. On this occasion, he is making a special effort to charm the children, whom he has so many times heard his beloved Miss Elizabeth mention with great fondness. Of course, who can blame a man madly in love if he acts upon some ulterior motive?

* * * * *

The business in London having been thus concluded, my master is now back at Pemberley.

Though my master was still away in London, the Hursts and Miss Bingley left for Scarborough upon the first of September as they had planned. It seems that Miss Bingley made not a little fuss and said she was not going, but Mrs Hurst reminded her sister of her duty by her relatives up north, and Miss Bingley finally agreed though with very little grace.

If I may be allowed to express my true sentiment about it, 'Good riddance!' is the phrase that readily comes to mind.

The other guests who came for the grouse season, too, left this morning, and now, Pemberley is quieter with only Mr Bingley left as a guest.

Everyone has now retired for the night, and my master is buried deep in thought, having now time and leisure of mind to reflect upon other matters. He is muttering to me again as usual, which is a special method he employs when he needs to think hard about something which needs sorting out in his own mind.

“Bingley ought to return to Netherfield,” he mutters into my fur. “I do not know whether or not Miss Bennet's love for Bingley still remains the same after all this time. But there was something in Miss Elizabeth's manner that gave me hope when she welcomed the chance to renew her acquaintance with Bingley on that occasion in August. Was it my wishful thinking that she seemed happy to sense Bingley's love for her sister still unchanged? Did she believe or even know that her sister's happiness still depended heavily upon Bingley's love? Oh, I hope so! Bingley ought to return to Netherfield. Oh, but how I shall rate myself if I find Miss Bennet's love for Bingley is no more!”

Chapter 17

* * * * *

My master and Mr Bingley are now relaxing in the library with a glass of brandy in their hands.

"Bingley, do you not think it is about time you visited Netherfield again? You have stayed away long enough," says my master, carrying out his plan.

"Oh, in fact I have been thinking the same thing," says Mr Bingley, clearly elated, but he tries to assume relative nonchalance. He, of course, still believes that my master totally disapproves of his love for Miss Bennet. He adds hurriedly, "Em... that is, I do not wish the neighbours to think that I am shunning their society. If I am to keep Netherfield, I will have to show some courtesy to them at least and show myself now and then."

Neither my master nor Mr Bingley mentions the Bennets, let alone Miss Bennet, my master wishing to avoid the discussion of her until he is sure of the present state of her sentiments towards Mr Bingley, and Mr Bingley not wishing my master to know that he still loves the lady as ardently as before.

* * * * *

Thus, it has been decided that they are to return to Netherfield as soon as the middle of the month. I am heartily looking forward to seeing Miss Elizabeth again.

I hope Mr Bingley's sisters will not decide that they should come down to Netherfield, too, hearing of the gentlemen's foray into Hertfordshire again. May they stay in Scarborough forever!

Chapter 17

Chapter 18

In which my master and Mr Bingley return to Hertfordshire

We arrived at Netherfield two evenings ago. Knowing how words spread though the countryside, both Mr Bingley and my master were certain that the locals would have heard of their arrival almost the moment their carriages turned into the neighbourhood.

Many a gentleman in the neighbourhood lost no time in renewing their acquaintance, and yesterday morning and this morning, came to pay their respects to Mr Bingley and my master. Mr Bennet, however, to Mr Bingley's great perturbance, was not one of them.

"Why has Mr Bennet not come?" wails Mr Bingley. "It has been two days. Surely he must have heard of my arrival. Mr Bennet must be irrevocably offended by the manner I left Netherfield last November. I left without even a word of farewell. He does not wish to know me any more! And even if he did not, if Mrs Bennet wished him to, she would surely have prevailed upon him. So, it must only mean that even Mrs Bennet is seriously displeased with me!"

From my master's silence and tortured face, I can only deduce that my master is of the same opinion.

* * * * *

"I have to do something to mitigate the evils that I visited upon Bingley," says my master to me, rubbing a hand across the back of his neck, as if the strain of the situation is taking a toll upon his shoulders. I suppose Mr Trent will be able to give some massage to him later.

"I should never have interfered with Bingley's love concern last November," my master continues. "Bingley is dithering. He would not listen to me when I say he should wait upon Mr Bennet rather than wait for Mr Bennet to wait upon him. He insists that he cannot be welcome, and that he will never find courage to show himself at Longbourn without being assured that they do not detest him. He is threatening to leave Netherfield, and that as early as tomorrow, and this time never to return! I seriously do not know what I can do. I myself have not the courage to lead Bingley boldly to Longbourn. It will be like a blind man leading a blind man and both will be sure to fall!" And my master holds his head in his hands, as if he is totally at his wit's end.

In my opinion, if my master just drags Mr Bingley to Longbourn by force or by coercion, everything will be perfectly fine. However, though it is not my place to say so, humans are damned troublesome creatures, and they sometimes do not seem to see the obvious.

* * * * *

I shall have to take the matter into my own hands. I shall have to do something, though I do not know what I can do at the moment. If I go out and wander around, I might hit upon some idea. Taking in abundant fresh air into one's lungs to deliver plenty of oxygen to one's brain can sometimes do wonders.

* * * * *

Not having been paying due attention to my surroundings while thinking hard what I should do, I seem to have travelled no less than three miles and inadvertently wandered into the Bennets' estate.

Suddenly, I espy hidden among the undergrowth a small hare snare, which must have been placed by Mr Bennet's gamekeeper, and a thought comes to mind.

Would I be able to make use of the snare somehow? What if ... what if I pretend to have been careless enough to have myself caught in the snare? It is well past noon now. If I remember rightly, Mr Bennet's gamekeeper always makes his daily patrol of the estate in the early afternoon. I am quite certain that he knows me, that is, knows me to be my master's dog. If the gamekeeper sees me caught in the snare ...

I cannot exactly predict what he will do, but the most likely scenario will surely be that he will inform Mr Bennet of it.

I would, however, hate to suffer pain unnecessarily, and arranging oneself to be caught in the snare deliberately but in such a way as not to cause oneself too much pain is a far trickier business than one would assume. In order to limit the injury to myself to the minimum, I should somehow try to manoeuvre the snare so that it will only catch the very end of my tail. I will try to make the snare snap shut by thumping my tail to release the spring.

Here it goes! Bloody Hell! Oh, pardon my language! I never expected it to be so painful! I have managed to have only my tail trapped. However, not just the very tiny tip of it as I planned, but a few inches of it! It is deuced painful! The length and trouble I have to go to for the sake of those two love-stricken gentlemen who cannot summon up courage! I think I deserve a good and juicy bone or two at least!

Now I have only to wait till Mr Bennet's gamekeeper comes along. It should not be long.

* * * * *

Here he comes! Wait! Someone else is with the gamekeeper.

To my great joy, I realize the other person to be Mr Bennet himself happening to be on patrol with his gamekeeper!

I yelp, feigning distress, and whine, raising my eyes and looking at their faces in turn in a fittingly pathetic, supplicatory fashion, which, I am sure, will not fail to inspire pity in their minds. Well, 'feigning distress' I say, but in point of fact, I am in some distress, if not in great distress.

"There, there, you naughty scamp! Whatever mischief have you been up to?" says Mr Bennet as if I were some shaggy rapscallion. "I seem to recall I have seen you somewhere before, though," adds Mr Bennet.

"If I'm not mistaken, sir," says the gamekeeper, "he is the dog belonging to that somewhat haughty gentleman, Mr Bingley's friend."

"Somewhat haughty gentleman? Mr Bingley's friend? Mr Darcy, you mean?" says Mr Bennet. "Yes, I do believe you are right! He does belong to him! So, that must mean Mr Darcy, too, as is rumoured, is back at Netherfield."

The gamekeeper releases my tail from the snare, and I see it is bleeding rather more profusely than I expected. I lick the wound clean and feel much better. Of course the wound is actually no cause for concern for a robust, well-exercised, healthy dog like me, and I could easily stand up and run, but I have rather a canning plan to compass my end. I assume the guise of being weak and somewhat overwrought by the trauma, and remain lying on the ground, whimpering in a most affecting 'dog in distress' manner.

"I presume I ought to take the dog back to Netherfield in my carriage, and apologise to Mr Darcy causing his dog injury," says Mr Bennet.

I almost feel like jumping up and running around, congratulating myself on my genius. But, no. Of course, I stay put, still feigning to be too weak to move.

Mr Bennet bids the gamekeeper carry me, who does as he is bidden. He lifts me and cradles me in his arms with unexpected tenderness for such a burly, uncouth looking man, taking great care not to put too much strain on my injured tail.

We come to where Mr Bennet's carriage stands.

"So, I shall be off to Netherfield, then," says Mr Bennet to the gamekeeper through the window of the carriage. "See to it that the veterinarian will be sent to Netherfield without delay. But make sure not to tell anything about it to anyone else, especially to Mrs Bennet. If Mrs Bennet finds out that your snare has injured the precious dog belonging to Mr Bingley's precious friend, you will be in her bad books. In the unlikely event that Mrs Bennet or my daughters should come to the gamekeeper's lodge and ask you of my whereabouts, just tell them you do not have a clue where I am. And in any event, I do not wish them to find out I have paid a visit to Mr Bingley. Mrs Bennet has been nagging me to do so, and I would be damned if she thought I would ever be at her beck and call. It will be much more fun to let her believe I will not visit him. Leave her in the dark."

So, it is exactly as I thought. Mrs Bennet is eager to renew her acquaintance with Mr Bingley, or to speak more precisely, she is eager for her eldest daughter to renew her acquaintance with him.

* * * * *

The carriage trundles towards Netherfield.

"This is indeed quite an favourable turn of events," Mr Bennet soliloquises. "I was thoroughly determined against calling on Mr Bingley at the behest of Mrs Bennet, but I must admit I have been feeling not a little guilty with regard to Jane, as Jane is my dear daughter and I do wish her happiness. But this gives me a splendid excuse for visiting Mr Bingley, and furthermore I shall have a highly legitimate reason for asking the gentlemen not to say anything of my visit to Mrs Bennet and my daughters."

Now the carriage arrives at Netherfield.

Mr Bingley's butler opens the door, and at Mr Bennet's request, a footman is called to carry me to the library where my master and Mr Bingley are at this moment relaxing.

After greetings of reacquaintance are exchanged, Mr Bennet makes a sincere apology to my master for causing me injury. Here, though, the task of bringing Mr Bennet to Netherfield accomplished, I consider the time has come for me to show them that my injury is nothing to be really concerned about. I stand up and walk to my master gingerly and very slowly, tentatively wagging my tail.

"Julius Caesar is a fully trained gun-dog," says my master patting my back, "and should have been able to eschew being caught in snares like those laid in the fields. I do not know what caused him to be so careless. So, please do not feel guilty about it, as the fault was as much Julius Caesar's, if not more, as it was your gamekeeper's. And as you see, he seems to be almost fine already. It must have been just the shock of being caught in the snare rather than the injury itself that made him so weak for a while."

Mr Bennet thanks my master for his leniency, and says he is relieved to see me looking fairly comfortable.

The veterinarian whom Mr Bennet arranged to be sent is arrived. He examines my tail, and an able animal doctor that he is, of course correctly assesses my condition immediately, and delivers the verdict that the injury which the snare has visited upon my tail is a very minor one. He even says he cannot at all see what made me so weak!

Thus assured by what the veterinarian has said, Mr Bennet puts aside the worries concerning my injury, and turns his attention to the more important matter, that is to say, the business of inducing the Netherfield gentlemen to visit Longbourn.

"The whole neighbourhood are much excited and elated, as indeed are all of us at Longbourn, that you are back in our midst at Netherfield," says Mr Bennet, looking at my master and Mr Bingley alternately, "and Mrs Bennet will consider it the highest honour to see you again at Longbourn. Indeed, she will be deeply hurt if you do not come, and I dearly hope you will visit us without delay. But I shall have to ask you one favour, if I may. You will oblige me greatly, if you could keep the whole of this business from my wife. If she ever finds out that my snare has injured Mr Darcy's precious dog, she will be unutterably displeased with my gamekeeper, and God knows what she will say! She might insist I dismiss him, and that would never do! I cannot do without him!"

Both my master and Mr Bingley give Mr Bennet their word that they will keep a strict silence about the business, and they with alacrity promise him that they will wait upon the ladies at Longbourn first thing tomorrow morning.

Everything settled thus to his satisfaction, Mr Bennet takes his leave, again asking for the two gentlemen's confirmation that they will call at Longbourn tomorrow morning but not utter a word about his visiting them to any of the ladies at Longbourn.

My master and Mr Bingley turn to me as soon as Mr Bennet is gone, and the expressions on their faces are absolutely beaming.

"Julius Caesar, old boy!" says my master, "you have done great service to Bingley! Your being caught in the snare was such a piece of good luck! Not that I make light of your injury, mind. But without Mr Bennet's firm assurance that he will receive a hearty welcome at Longbourn, Bingley would never have had enough courage to visit them."

"Indeed, Julius Caesar, you are my saviour! What would I have done without you!" says Mr Bingley and hugs me ever so tightly.

I humbly accept the accolade.

* * * * *

Both my master and Mr Bingley, clearly in fits of the fidgets, rose much earlier than their normal practice this morning. In fact almost with the sun, I should say, and I am not exaggerating.

Both gentlemen are pacing back and forth in the library till the suitable time arrives for the planned morning visit to Longbourn. Not allowed into the secret of my master's fixated love for Miss Elizabeth, Mr Bingley is much puzzled by my masters restlessness.

"Why on earth are you, too, so agitated, Darcy?" asks Mr Bingley.

"Watching you pace in that fashion, Bingley, does make me, too, feel oddly nervous in sympathy," my master answers mendaciously.

"Oh, I do beg you pardon," says Mr Bingley, "but I cannot help it. It is deuced nerve-racking."

* * * * *

Chapter 18

My master and Mr Bingley are nearing Longbourn on their horses with me tagging along behind them. Their progress is slow denoting the degree of their cowering agitation.

I glimpse a female figure at one of the windows, and look hard. I see at once that the figure belongs to Mrs Bennet and she has seen the two gentlemen approaching, though the said gentlemen do not seem to have noticed it at all. She clasps her hands as if in great elation, and a moment later disappears from the window.

"Girls, girls! Mr Bingley is coming! Mr Bingley is here!" I can almost hear Mrs Bennet's voice ringing though the house. "Oh, Jane, Jane, how regrettable it is that you have not dressed yourself in that fine morning dress of the colour of a blushing rose, which is so very becoming! It is vexing that there is no time for you to change your apparel!"

The two gentlemen have now arrived at the house.

Mrs Bennet is clearly so overjoyed to renew her acquaintance with Mr Bingley that she just stands there broadly smiling but mute, with her be-ringed hand over her heart as if the sheer joy of seeing Mr Bingley again at her premises has made her speechless. But the moment of unprecedented speechlessness passing, she becomes even more noisily solicitous to him than before, and Mr Bingley, though he is relieved and unutterably happy, is as always overwhelmed by her tremendous volubility. But in stark contrast, Mrs Bennet's attitude towards my master is as standoffish as ever and there remains much to be improved.

* * * * *

A few days have passed since the visit to Longbourn, and in his own all too subtle way, my master seems to have been trying ever so hard to be near Miss Elizabeth, to talk to her, and to convey his sentiments to her, but very little has come about so far.

At the several dinner parties which have been held in honour of the two gentlemen who have returned to Netherfield, Mr Bingley has been fortunate enough to be often seated with Miss Bennet next to him, which I strongly suspect, has been with Mrs Bennet's contrivance. But my master has had no such luck. He has more often than not been placed as far removed from Miss Elizabeth as the size of the table allowed, which might also have been by the ministration of Mrs Bennet, who still seems to believe in her second daughter's persisting hatred of my master.

And now, having come back from one of such dinner parties, my master as usual is talking to me about it.

For once, he seems to have had the great luck of being seated next to Miss Elizabeth today.

"But alas!" cries my master. "As luck would have it, the seat on the other side of me was occupied by Mrs Richards, who is even fonder of talking than Mrs Bennet, and I was obliged to listen to her ceaseless chatter all the time, which gave me very little leeway to talk to Miss Elizabeth! Of course, if I had been so minded, I could have shunned Mrs Richards, never minding offending the lady, and used this great opportunity to talk to Miss Elizabeth. But, Julius Caesar, you know what I am! I am utterly useless! The more I wish to talk, the less able I seem to become. I feel deuced self-conscious and cannot think of anything to say! I never would have imagined I would ever envy anything of Wickham, but I wish now that I had his silvery tongue!"

But it seems my master is not alone in this folly of not being able to talk, and Miss Elizabeth has been, too, unusually reticent herself to him since he returned to Hertfordshire. Which does not help him at all, and is making it even harder for him to fathom her sentiments towards him.

Mrs Bennet's attitude towards my master still has not improved one whit, it seems. But despite her obvious dislike of my master, Mrs Bennet has always been surprisingly kind to me. She must be a great animal lover, and apparently, the proverb 'he who hates Peter harms his dog' does not apply in her case. For which I am truly grateful, but I hope she will be a little kinder to my master as well.

My master, though he has, quite understandably, often been a little piqued by Mrs Bennet's all too unsubtly discourteous attitude towards him, has ever been sensible for her kindness towards me. And I have once heard him say, "Mrs Bennet, admittedly, is awfully silly, vulgar and unceremoniously rude to me, but I cannot quite hate her when she is so nice to you, Julius Caesar. We should always count our blessings."

* * * * *

My master has some urgent business to attend to in London and is to go there tomorrow for some ten days' visit.

He is very reluctant to leave Hertfordshire – or more to the point, loath to leave Miss Elizabeth at this critical time. But the appointment being one of great importance as well as long standing, he cannot bring himself to abandon the obligation however burdensome.

One thing which has been weighing heavily on my master's mind for some time is that he has still not told Mr Bingley that he did wrong in separating Mr Bingley from Miss Bennet last November. So he has decided to make a clean breast of it all before leaving for London and to encourage Mr Bingley to follow his heart.

* * * * *

"I have some matter of importance I wish to talk to you about, Bingley," thus my master opens the topic.

"What is it? That sounds rather sombre. You make me nervous," says Mr Bingley a little anxiously.

"Tell me truthfully, Bingley. You, I believe, are still in love with Miss Bennet. Am I not right?"

"Umm ..." Mr Bingley hesitates, presumably thinking that my master will not approve. But, "Yes... yes, I am," he admits finally. "I know you will think me pitiable, Darcy, to be still hankering after her against your advice after all this time. But yes, I still love her. Believe me, I honestly tried and tried to forget her!"

"And to think I nearly destroyed both your and Miss Bennet's chance of happiness!" cries my master.

"Eh? You nearly destroyed both Miss Bennet's happiness and mine? Whatever do you mean?"

"Only this. I told you last year that I believed Miss Bennet did not return your love, and advised you to part with her. I did great wrong to interfere. I dared to consider myself someone who knew better than you. That was downright arrogance. But in my defence, I beg you to believe me when I say that I did really think at the time she did not love you and marrying her would never lead you to happiness. But I was utterly mistaken. I have found since, Bingley, that Miss Bennet did truly love you then. And I firmly believe she still does."

"Miss Bennet loved me, and still does? But, wait! Do I really understand what you are trying to say? How on earth can you say she loved me? You have never been in the position to know that."

"Bingley, it was Miss Elizabeth who told me."

"Miss Elizabeth told you!" cries Mr Bingley in sheer wonder. "But how can it have been? How did such a thing come about?"

"Bingley, I know you are soon to ask Miss Bennet for her hand in marriage, and she will accept you. And you will almost certainly hear of this from her someday, as I have no doubt Miss Elizabeth would have told her dearest sister and confidante about this. So, I will tell you honestly. I think you remember my telling you that I met Miss Elizabeth when I went to Rosings last April."

Mr Bingley nods assent.

"I... asked her to be my wife then, but was rejected," says my master.

"Eh~!?" Mr Bingley lets out an incredulous screech? "You, proposed to Miss Elizabeth, but was rejected!? God God, Darcy! But surely you did not love Miss Elizabeth!"

"You are wrong, Bingley. I have loved her dearly almost from the first moment I met her," my master adds.

"Eh~!? Goodness gracious!" Mr Bingley gives out an even louder screech again. "You hid that remarkably well, Darcy! Of course, when you asked Miss Elizabeth to dance with you at the Netherfield ball, I was not a little amazed to be honest, and thought what a rare thing it was for you to ask anyone but the closest acquaintances to dance with you. But fancy Miss Elizabeth rejecting your suit! I would never have believed there existed anyone who would dare to say 'No' to you!"

"One of the reasons she gave me then why she would not have me was that I had ruined her loving sister's dearest wish for happiness, that is, in relation to you."

"But in that case, why did she not blame me? Surely, anybody would have thought I was the one who was by far the most blameable. I do not understand. And how could she have known that you persuaded me against Miss Bennet?"

"Oh, I do not know how she came by that fact, but presumably she just guessed it. Knowing how utterly smitten you had been by Miss Bennet, she could easily have deduced that you would never have given her up without some strong pressure from your friends, and in her eyes the friend with the strongest influence upon you must have been me."

"Darcy, I feel not a little guilty about having been the cause for Miss Elizabeth's disapprobation of you."

"Oh, you need not feel responsible for it at all. There were plenty other reasons as well, I assure you. But I am hoping that she has reassessed those reasons and has now amended her view of me a little. I do at least feel now that she no longer sees me as the repulsive ogre of a man that she thought I was back in April."

"Oh, Darcy! I am sure she will come to love you once she knows the real you!"

"That I can only hope."

"Darcy, pardon me for asking a strange question, but did you happen to be carrying around a miniature of Miss Elizabeth during the season?"

"Huh? How on earth did you know that?"

"So, it was true! There was a rumour flying around that you ever and anon took out a miniature of a lady from your coat pocket and looked at it in a most loving and yet infinitely pensive fashion. It was indeed the talk of the *ton*. But when Hurst told me about it, I just dismissed it as a silly talk."

"Well, I never knew I was seen! And I thought I was being very cautious!"

Chapter 18

Chapter 19

In which my master goes up to London, where he is given a ray of hope

Leaving his heart in Hertfordshire, my master travelled to Town. He has had a hectic week. It is now the middle of the afternoon of the seventh day, and my master is enjoying a few hours of rare relaxation. Three more days, and he will be able to return to Hertfordshire, to Miss Elizabeth.

The front knocker sounds loud and impetuously several times, and a few moments later, I hear Mrs Henderson, my master's London housekeeper, answer the door.

The hall resounds with a loud, irascible female voice.

'Curiosity' is my second name. I hurry to the hall to do a little bit of reconnoitring.

“Where is Darcy!? Where is my nephew!?” the voice peals like a clap of thunder. I instantly recognize the voice of my master's aunt, Lady Catherine de Bourgh. Lady Catherine arriving thus suddenly without any pre-warning ... I smell trouble.

I have often heard people say 'looking like thunder', but now, for the first time, I truly understand what the expression means. Lady

Catherine indeed has a face that the Norse god of thunder, Thor, would have been immensely proud of.

Seeing me, her bad-tempered face becomes even more thunderous. I have no idea where that ill humour of hers has derived from or who is to be at the receiving end of it. But in the light of the fact that she has travelled here thus unexpectedly, that her ire will be directed to my master seems to be a foregone conclusion.

As I might have mentioned several times before, I am of the breed English Setter, the breed known to be of a disposition so friendly and mild as to be trusted in the presence of even babies and small children. And I, although I say it myself, am the epitome of the trustworthy breed, and am forever good-natured and kind.

But, 'Protectiveness' is my third name.

Protecting my master from harm is the task I take most seriously. If my master were to be confronted by a rough customer, I would fight to an inch of my life for my master, and he who fights on the other side of me would be sure to find me a fierce opponent.

But Lady Catherine, as might be expected, is a completely different story. She is my master's aunt after all, and with however little favour she might be regarded by her nephew, for such as me to be showing disrespect or displeasure, let alone aggression towards her, would be most improper. The most I could do would be to seize an opportunity to hinder her from barging her way into my master's presence in her thus vitriolic mood.

I woof lightly just once first to test the water, then, try grabbing hold of the hem of her gown and, growling in a half-hearted fashion, tug it to stop her progress to my master's library.

But Lady Catherine is a formidable foe. She does not at all take my meddling kindly, and kicking me out of the way with her foot without ceremony, and I would say, with somewhat unladylike violence, which nearly knocks the air out of my lungs, strides towards my master's library looking like the very picture of a Fury, a dread goddess. She yanks open the door to the library with tremendous force. At the sound of the violent opening of the door, my master turns round in his chair, then stands up.

"There you are, Darcy!" all but bellows Lady Catherine. "I would have thought you should have proper enough manners at least to come out to greet your aunt!"

Judging from his expression, my master is in a greatest state of flabbergastation. Given so sudden an arrival of his not awfully beloved aunt, and her mood apparently even more foul than usual, it is a completely understandable reaction.

"I do beg your pardon," says my master, almost stuttering, "for my lack of manners, but I had no notion that you were here, as I was not at all expecting you to be honouring me with your visit today."

"Humph!" Lady Catherine grunts. "That is hardly a good enough reason for your incivility!"

In my humble opinion, it most certainly is a good enough reason, but my master knows better than to gainsay whatever Lady Catherine is pleased to proclaim, and says nothing. He gestures to offer his aunt a seat, which she accepts and sits herself down. And then, my master, too, takes a seat.

Lady Catherine looks at my master's face, apparently anticipating him to inquire the purport of her visit. But my master rigidly maintains his silence. After a while, Lady Catherine seems to become not a little exasperated at his reticence, or rather, his lack of interest.

"Have you no curiosity?" demands Lady Catherine. "Do you not wish to hear why I am here? You sorely lack in spirit of enquiry, Darcy!"

Thus reproached, my master cannot but say, "To what do I owe the pleasure of your visit?" The query is made without evident assiduity, but politely enough, exhibiting his tremendous skill at disguising his emotions which I often marvel at.

"Give me time to take some breaths first. You should at least show that much solicitousness to your ageing aunt," says the contrarian extraordinaire testily. Nothing and nobody can please this cross-grained termagant.

It is a great wonder that my master can stop himself from heaving a huffing sigh of irritation. He waits silently and patiently till his aunt discards her contrariness at her pleasure.

A couple of minutes elapses and Lady Catherine appears to think she has made my master wait long enough.

"So, Darcy, you must be all-agog to discover what has brought your beloved aunt all the way here," asserts Lady Catherine.

My master nods assent, deciding, I suspect, that there is no point in declaring that he couldn't care less why she is here as long as she removes herself the moment she finishes her business.

"Brought to my notice two days ago was an alarming report," thus commences Lady Catherine, "which told me that you, Darcy – a scion, though not of the direct line, of one of the noblest houses dating back to the reign of Henry the Fifth – have lost yourself to your baser instinct to such an extent as to let yourself be fallen prey to a calculating, lowly adventuress, and to allow yourself to be cozened into even becoming engaged to the conniving vulture! What have you got to say to that!?"

"A report of my becoming involved with an adventuress?" says my master incredulously. "Where on earth has such an absurd rumour originated?"

"So, it is a lie," Lady Catherine heaves a great sigh of relief.

"Surely, you did not even for a moment give credence to such a tale," says my master reprovingly.

"Of course, I did not!" protests Lady Catherine. "That is why I went to see the girl to demand she renege such a claim!"

"You went to see the girl!?" master all but gasps in utter shock. "So, she is someone known to you?"

"Yes, that is gratitude for you! This girl, the adventuress, in return for the great kindness I bestowed upon her in Kent, must have conspired and plotted with her family to gain her end and spread the false rumour of your involvement with her to place you, my beloved nephew, in an disadvantageous position where you might be obliged to offer her your hand in marriage. But she clearly had not bargained for me, who would interfere and denounce such a rumour to spoil her plan."

"Your kindness to this girl in Kent?" says my master, beginning to feel some unease and dread. "Whom, pray, do you mean when you say 'this girl, the adventuress'?"

"Why, Miss Elizabeth Bennet, of course! Who else!?" spits Lady Catherine.

"Miss Elizabeth Bennet!?" this time, my master veritably screeches.

"Do not shout! Shouting is so vulgar!" says Lady Catherine, herself shouting far louder than my master.

"It cannot have been Miss Elizabeth who spread the rumour! She would never do such a thing!" my master protests.

"Fustian! Who else would there be to have a better reason to do so? But of course, the scheming, mendacious woman that she is, she denied it all!"

"You do not mean that you went and accused Miss Elizabeth of such iniquity to her face! Surely, you did not!"

"Of course I did!" retorts Lady Catherine. "Which was no more than what she deserved! Such a despicable intrigante had to be shown that she would not deceive anybody with her audacious lies, and should be taught to know her place and be told unreservedly that she would never be accepted into a family of such noble standing and lineage as yours! She admitted to me that she was not engaged to you, which was a great relief, but when I demanded that she give me her word never to go into such an engagement in the future, she flatly refused to do so, and that, in a most outrageously insolent manner! I had never been treated in such a shabby fashion in my life! She even made it abundantly clear that, if you really were to make an offer to her, she would consider herself wholly qualified to accept your hand, if not in those exact words! She fully signified, Darcy, that she is determined to have you! Now what have you to say?"

My master looks stunned. Which is quite understandable.

Miss Elizabeth refusing to promise Lady Catherine never to become engaged to my master!? Miss Elizabeth saying that, if my master were to make an offer to her, she would consider herself wholly qualified to accept his hand!? Does it not mean that there is a great possibility that she now regards my master in quite a favourable light, or... even loves him? Does it not mean that my master's suit will have a much better chance the second time?

The Miss Elizabeth of last April would have gladly promised Lady Catherine never even to set her eyes upon my master ever again, and I would not have at all been surprised if she had even gone so far as to declare that she wished him to be thrown into the fires of Hades.

Lady Catherine seems to take my master's stunned silence as a horrified reaction to the manner Miss Elizabeth behaved.

"Aye, aye, Darcy, no wonder you have been stunned into silence," she says, nodding her head in a self-satisfied, self-congratulatory fashion. "Such vulgarity in a woman would have given any gentleman a feeling of disgust. Putting herself forward in such a brazen fashion! If you were to make an offer to her, indeed! She would consider herself fully qualified to accept you? Poppycock! What presumption! What audacity! I have never heard of anything so preposterous!"

Buried deep in his own thoughts, my master seems to be only half listening to what his aunt is rabbiting on about.

"I am wholly gratified that you appear to be feeling as horrified as I am with this business," says Lady Catherine approvingly.

My master keeps silent. He seems to decide that it will suit his purpose better to leave his aunt in that delusion and not to undeceive her, which I applaud as a very sensible decision. If Lady Catherine should have even an inkling of my master's true sentiments toward Miss Elizabeth, hell would break loose, and my master would be seared to cinders. Better to let a sleeping dragon lie. At least for the time being.

"Ah, the hour is much further advanced than I have imagined!" cries out Lady Catherine as if panicked, glancing at the clock upon the mantelpiece. "I should take my leave immediately! I know you would have wished your beloved aunt to stay the night, but I shall have to disappoint you, as I must needs be back in Kent tonight. And in any event, I do not particularly find it congenial to stay here these days, as, whenever I stay, your accursed dog will disturb me in the middle of the night and prevent me from having a peaceful sleep! How many times have I been suddenly shaken to wakefulness by the cursed dog throwing himself onto my bed and sometimes even howling like a mad dog in his sleep? I have lost count! I do not know why he finds my bed so attractive to sleep on. It is a wonder the dog refuses to learn that he is not wanted, because I do always show my displeasure and disgust amply and clearly. You need to train your dog better, Darcy!"

I know how my master dreads the thought of this aunt of his who is so difficult to please staying at his house, so every time she does, I do my very utmost to render her stay as unpalatable to her as possible.

My master, I spy with my little eye, is now immensely relieved that his aunt is leaving, and is making a diligent endeavour to prevent his smiles escaping. I feel rather proud of my contribution. But here is a most difficult task that my master has to perform. He cannot show his elation too openly and plainly as the contrary aunt will be sure to take umbrage, and just to spite him, might decide to stay after all. He has to pretend that he is regretful that she has to leave. But under no circumstances should he overdo the regret lest she should take it at its face value, which might well put the totally misinformed idea into her head that she should stay for her dear nephew's sake. It is a question of delicate balance.

But my master is quite an old hand at handling this troublesome aunt of his, and delivers the act very convincingly to satisfy her ego to just the right degree.

* * * * *

Lady Catherine gone, my master heaves a deep sigh of relief.

"You are ever my lifesaver," says my master to me, though I think it rather an exaggeration. "You have to endeavour to disturb her sleep whenever she stays!"

My master's head is filled with the happy possibility that Miss

Elizabeth might return his love. He seems to be recapitulating over and over again in his mind what his aunt told him. He hugs me tight, mumbling into my fur, as he always does while he cogitates.

"Can it be really true that Miss Elizabeth refused to promise never to become engaged to me? Can she really have said she considers herself every bit entitled to accept me? Dear Julius Caesar, what can it mean? Can it truly be what I am thinking? I am afraid of allowing myself to have hope but I am only human. How can I stop myself!?" thus my master debates and redebates with himself, mumbling. "Oh, would that the business were complete and I could hurry back to Hertfordshire tomorrow! But I have three more long days yet to endure in London!"

Chapter 19

Chapter 20

In which my master is back in Hertfordshire, where he pops the question for the second time

His business in Town finally concluded, my master has hurried back to Netherfield.

Mr Bingley, who has been impatiently waiting for my master's return to impart to my master the conclusion of his love concern, loses no time to do so. My master is overjoyed to be informed that, as he correctly anticipated, Mr Bingley's suit has been eagerly welcomed and blissfully accepted by everyone at Longbourn. Mr Bingley declares himself to be the most fortunate of men alive upon earth.

Do I sense my master's mind immediately turn to the impending business of the greatest moment of his own, to wit, proposing to Miss Elizabeth the second time? Decidedly I do, and I can almost hear his heart leap into his throat and then start to flutter in the funniest of ways, as one's heart is known to have the decided tendency to do so when one grows nervous.

Tomorrow, when Mr Bingley visits Longbourn in the morning to spend the day there, which he says has been his daily practice since his engagement, my master will accompany him and bolster up courage to pop the question again.

I rather suspect that in such cases as these, one should just try to relax and have a good night's sleep before the momentous day, but well... that is a tall order, if there ever were one, to ask of my master.

* * * * *

The two Netherfield gentlemen set out to Longbourn as early as it could possibly be considered proper, to present themselves before the Bennet ladies, one with the apparent air of a man visiting his affianced, confident of the welcome he will receive, and the other less confident, who has once been rejected and is about to trust his luck to God the second time. Of course, nobody who might catch sight of my master would ever suspect him of being a man lacking in confidence at any time as his air is ever assured and collected. But I, who have far superior sensory perception to humans in every conceivable arena, can detect how unusually nervous and diffident my master is on this occasion.

“I have hit upon a capital idea!” says Mr Bingley upon the way to Longbourn. “I have always hoped to be alone with Jane without the rather cumbersome chaperonage of Mrs Bennet. Julius Caesar being with us today will give us a most convenient, highly plausible excuse for taking a walk abroad today. I very much doubt that Mrs Bennet will join our walk as Jane has more than once told me that her mother is not a good walker and actually abhors walking.”

Good Lord, Mr Bingley has suddenly gained such confidence now that he is engaged, and he even calls Miss Bennet 'Jane'!

My master, who knows that Miss Elizabeth is a great walker, and therefore is most likely to welcome the idea of a little exercise, agrees with Mr Bingley promptly.

I am more than happy to be of use as a pretext.

“It is a beauteous autumn day abroad, and it is indeed a great pity to waste such a day being cooped up indoors. What say you all about taking a walk? Darcy's dog, Julius Caesar, being always full of beans, will be very happy to run around outside, and we should like to indulge him if you are all amenable," so suggests the newly confident Mr Bingley as soon as we arrive at Longbourn.

I, in token of my appreciation and gratification, woof once cheerily and wag my tail vigorously, though people would no doubt assume I do so only because I have heard my name uttered.

Miss Bennet, Miss Elizabeth and Miss Catherine, as we anticipated, prove themselves to be most willing to take part, whereas Mrs Bennet, to the profoundest, secret relief of both the gentlemen, declines to be of the party. Miss Mary also declines, saying she cannot spare the time as she has an awful lot of practice to do on the piano.

Thus, the three ladies and the two gentlemen set out to enjoy a constitutional walk around the area.

Mr Bingley and Miss Bennet rather dawdle along the lane, and soon, whether deliberately or inadvertently, though I firmly believe it is the former, begin to let themselves fall far behind the others, and Miss Elizabeth, Miss Catherine and my master walk on together.

Miss Catherine is decidedly *de trop*. If she can be got rid of, my master can be alone with Miss Elizabeth and may be able to have the matter between them progress further. I have to think of some method to be rid of Miss Catherine.

We are soon to reach the fork of the lane, the right hand side of which leads to Lucas Lodge. If I could think up something – something to make Miss Catherine wish to visit the Lucas Lodge ...

I think hard and look hard at Miss Catherine's apparel, wondering if there is something I could make use of.

I see the trimmings adorning the hem of her dress a little loose at one place. As Miss Catherine stops and lowers herself to pluck a flower, I see a capital opportunity. I covertly insert my paw through the loosened loop and wait till Miss Catherine again raises herself. The result is far better than I have anticipated! That part of the trimmings fortuitously comes loose as the loop unravels, though not without a ripping sound alarmingly loud to my guilty ear, and as a result a good few inches of the material hangs free from the hem of the dress.

I quickly withdraw my paw and jump right back, fearful that Miss Catherine has heard the ripping sound. But Miss Catherine does not show any immediate reaction.

I cogitate for a second whether or not I should bark to alert Miss Catherine. Miss Catherine, however, obviously having felt or heard something, after a moment or two with delayed reaction, tries to crane her neck to look at the back of her dress, and notices the calamity.

"Oh, good Lord!" she gives out a small scream. "My trimmings are undone! However can it have happened?"

I glance askance at her face, and feel relieved that she seems to have no suspicion whatsoever that I was the culprit who occasioned the calamity. Though I am certain she would not have had the courage to chastise me in front of my master whom she is apparently in awe of, it would still have been a little awkward had she realized it.

"I should have them stitched on as soon as possible," says Miss Catherine, "before the damage spreads! How fortunate it is that Lucas Lodge is nearby! Would you mind terribly, Lizzy, if I part from you here to seek help from Maria Lucas? She will certainly be kind enough to assist me in mending the trimmings."

Miss Elizabeth has no objection, and judging from her face, she is not at all loath to be left alone with my master. My master is elated, which, to me, is as plain as the nose on my face, or should I say 'the snout', although I would say the strong emotion may well not be manifest to the human eye.

Miss Catherine bobs a curtsy to my master, and then is gone, and Miss Elizabeth and my master resume walking. There is a momentary silence. I secretly will my master to take this opportunity and boldly proceed on to that all-important business.

But my master is as tardy as ever, and to my despair, the one to break the ice is Miss Elizabeth.

"Mr Darcy, I am a very selfish creature and for the sake of giving relief to my own feelings, care not how much I may be wounding yours," thus she commences in a somewhat agitated manner.

Oh, God, no! What is this? Does she plan to give my master an ultimatum?

The colour drains from my master's face and he looks dejected. Surely, she cannot mean to reject him even before she gives him chance to pour out his undying love for her! Do not tell me my so far infallible senses have failed me at this important juncture of time! I cannot believe it! I am sure what I sense emanating from her person is amity ... or rather, if I may be bold, I would call it something more, something verging upon love, if not as profound and ardent as that which my master nurtures for her. I am certain of it!

But wait! She proceeds on to say something else!

She wishes to thank my master. For his great kindness to her sister, Miss Lydia. She knows it all. Mrs Gardiner is not to blame for breaking the promise not to divulge the secret. Because Miss Lydia was the one who let on the truth of his deep involvement in the business first.

Phew! Thank God! Miss Elizabeth's intention, when she said she cared not how much she might be wounding my master's feelings, was not to reject my master! It was, if I may say so, an odd way of phrasing it and a little misleading, but when one is nervous, one sometimes does not choose words carefully and says something a little muddlesome. She must have merely meant that, by thanking him, she would hurt his feelings, as it would reveal that she had discovered what he had desired to keep from the Bennets, namely, it had not been her uncle as they were led to believe who had found her sister and settled everything, but it was he, an outsider.

My master's countenance which became pallid and was the picture of anguish a moment ago, has regained its colour.

Miss Elizabeth thanks my master again and again in the name of all her family for his compassion and generosity, and the trouble he went through for her family's honour and happiness.

"If you will thank me, let it be for yourself alone." says my master. "I thought only of you."

Yes, Master, that is exactly the way to go! I silently congratulate him.

Chapter 20

And then, "Soldier on, Master! Take this opportunity and tell Miss Elizabeth how ardently you still love her!" I pray and urge my master on in my mind.

Whether or not my mute prayer has been conveyed, my master boldly proceeds. He vows his undying love for Miss Elizabeth and still unaltered wish for her hand in marriage, and asks her to tell him so at once if her feelings are still what they were last April, as that will silence him forever upon the subject.

I peek at Miss Elizabeth's face, and see at once a highly auspicious sign. She looks awfully embarrassed, but Miss Elizabeth of last April would never have looked like that! She might have blushed then, too, but that would have been a blush of anger, not the rosy blush of maidenly embarrassment of the present occasion. There is no denying she is flushed and awfully embarrassed, but she is decidedly melted with happiness!

Her distinctive boldness a little diminished and her usual articulacy somewhat impaired, Miss Elizabeth slowly but surely explains that her sentiments toward my master have made a complete about-turn since April, and that she receives his present assurance of love with profound gratitude and great joy, which, in my humble opinion, is in point of fact a declaration of love.

My master wished to keep the part he played in the affair of Miss Lydia and Mr Wickham from the Bennets, partly because he thought it would pain them if they found that their shameful secret was known to him, but the main reason was that he was fearful that he might put Miss Elizabeth in such a position as to make her feel herself indebted to my master if and when my master proposed to her the second time.

But even my master, who is normally very slow at that kind of thing, does seem able to see in Miss Elizabeth's countenance a genuine love for him and real happiness in receiving his love.

Good Heavens! I have never seen my master become so animated before with such a profusion of emotions! His noble patrician face normally stoical and lacking vibrancy is now suffused with rapture, which would be seen by anyone who has eyes to see, and his deep baritone voice usually level and solemn is now buoyant with joy, which would be heard by anyone who has ears to hear!

And Miss Elizabeth, who is always vivacious and courageous, is uncharacteristically bashful, with her flushed face hidden by the brim of her bonnet, and can barely raise her eyes to look at my master's face, which I think is the most beautiful picture I could ever imagine. Seeing in my master's face the look of the unutterable happiness I have so long hoped to see, my vision would have begun to blur by now with warm tears of gladness were I a human. But as I might have said before, we dogs do not cry in the same way as the humans do.

They walk on, though neither of them can be even remotely described as talking eloquently. In fact, they talk stutteringly by fits and starts at first, though they gradually come to find comfort in each other's company and their discourse begins to flow a little more smoothly upon various topics.

Then, after the long discourse, their gait begins markedly to slow down and finally comes to a halt. My master turns to Miss Elizabeth, and she, too, slowly turns to face my master. Miss Elizabeth looks at my master's face, and some expression there seems suddenly to make her awfully shy and she lowers her gaze.

Is my master going to ...

I, in order not to make them feel self-conscious, decide to make myself scarce, and go behind a thick bush, from whence I can see them perfectly well with my superior eyesight, but their inferior eyes will not be able to penetrate the dense bush.

My master steps closer to Miss Elizabeth, and tenderly draws her to him. Miss Elizabeth seems willing to be embraced and buries her flushed face in his bosom. My master holds her in his arms his cheek upon her head for a long while.

I can almost hear their loud heartbeats merging.

I know my master is a man of rectitude and propriety, sometimes much too much so, but these are extenuating circumstances. If an engaged couple (though not yet known to her family) cannot indulge themselves in a moment of passion, who could? I secretly urge my master in my mind to have the courage to forge another step forward.

There! My master softly places his fingers under Miss Elizabeth's chin, tilts her face upwards, and slowly lowers his face. He tenderly touches her lips with his lips. Oh, the soft caresses of their lips! What a beauteous picture it is to behold!

My master after the kiss, remains holding Miss Elizabeth for a long while more, as if he cannot bear to let her go, and Miss Elizabeth seems as happy to remain held in my master's strong arms as he is happy to have her there.

But of course, they cannot remain in that situation forever. My master reluctantly let her go, and they resume their walking.

My master offers his arm to her, and she looks up and smiles her shy but loving smile and takes it with a maidenly blush but without an unduly missish hesitation.

I see in Miss Elizabeth's face a genuine glow of blissful happiness, and again feel nearly brought to gladdened tears.

"Miss Bennet ... eh, may I call you Elizabeth?" my master asks.

"Of course!" says Miss Elizabeth, "I would be sad if you did not."

"Then, my dear Elizabeth," says my master with a smile, and suddenly reaches to his coat pocket and from thence produces something, "I have a confession to make."

"A confession? That sounds awfully serious," says Miss Elizabeth, feigning to be shocked, but with a comical raise of her eyebrows very characteristic to her.

"Yes," my master says, still smiling. "I am afraid that you might think I took a great liberty. I secretly had this likeness of you taken at the Netherfield ball last November."

Oh, oh, damnation! His treasured miniature of Miss Elizabeth! She will tell my master that I showed it to her in Kent, and then what will happen? My master will wonder how that could ever have happened!

"Oh, this miniature! I have already seen it, though just once," says Miss Elizabeth as predicted, to my great perturbation! I hope she will refrain from mentioning my name, though I rather think it is too much to hope for.

"You have already seen it!? But ... how can it be possible?" asks my master, justifiably stupefied.

"Julius Caesar brought it to me in Kent," Miss Elizabeth, alas, spills the beans, "after you gave me that long letter in which you explained everything. He also brought me a letter from Mr Wickham to you, in which he thanked you for a pecuniary advancement of three thousand pounds in exchange for the living."

Damn! I wish I could sink through the floor, but as it is, there is no floor to sink through. I feel like decamping and there are plenty of places I could go and hide, but on second thoughts, I ought to wait and see what my master's reaction will be. Will he be angry with me?

"Julius Caesar? Brought the miniature and the letter to you in Kent?" my master parrots, in an utterly bamboozled voice. "However did he manage to do that?"

"Oh, you know what pets are like," says Miss Elizabeth in an amused tone. "They are sometimes so naughty. They take a fancy to something and however many times we chide them, they would persist in meddling with it. My cat is always doing the same."

My master laughs and says he agrees without reservation that pets are sometimes deuced naughty. I feel a little insulted.

"Oh, but, please do not be cross with Julius Caesar," says Miss Elizabeth. "At that time, your letter had already shown me how stupid I had been and how unforgivably I had wronged you because of my former unreasonable prejudices, but I think the miniature and Mr Wickham's letter were the *coup de grâce*. The miniature made me realize how you had cared for me from such an early stage of our acquaintance, and I was filled with gratitude. I berated myself for injuring someone who had loved me with such tenderness. And Mr Wickham's letter was the confirmation of what you had told me in your letter. Although I think I would have come to believe your words without that confirmation, it certainly helped me to see sense sooner."

"So, I have to thank Julius Caesar for giving me the important succour. He well deserves a reward," says my master looking at me with an unusual, mischievous light in his eyes. "Do you know, Miss Elizabeth, sometimes I almost suspect that Julius Caesar in truth understands far more than we humans give him credit for."

"Oh, yes, I feel exactly the same," accents Miss Elizabeth. "I have so often thought that he wears such a sagacious look on his face. And I am certain that he loves his master as dearly as the most faithful of anybody's friends would."

"And I have for sometime been convinced that he loves you, too, as much as he loves me, or even more," says my master. "I have more than once had this uncanny feeling that Julius Caesar was making great efforts to matchmake for me."

Well, my master has been more perspicacious than I have given him credit for! Miss Elizabeth laughs one of her bell-like laughs, and says,

"Yes, I must admit that, back in April in Kent, when he brought this miniature and the letter and showed them to me with such an earnest expression in his face, I almost had this eerie notion that he was pleading to me for his master's sake!"

"I wonder if he really was," says my master in a rather pondering fashion, and he and Miss Elizabeth slowly turn their eyes to me with somewhat queer, unnervingly scrutinizing looks in their eyes.

Gracious Heaven! I cannot let them know or even suspect that I understand everything! If they did, they would behave in a much more guarded manner in front of me and would never divulge their innermost thoughts to me, and that would never do! I need to divert their attention from whatever suspicion they might have formed!

My biggest pleasure in life is to be able to see and listen to humans at their most private and truthful. If that pleasure were to be taken away from me, I would be utterly devastated!

So, I pretend not to have understood a thing, and casually continue along the path, now rushing to sniff this bush on the right in a doggy, inquisitive fashion, now running to examine that flower on the left in wise of a guileless dog, and ever and anon making my mark at the foot of tree trunks, looking the picture of innocence, I hope, as dogs are known to do.

"I suppose we are thinking too much," says my master, watching me nonchalantly meandering. "Julius Caesar certainly is an uncommonly intelligent fellow, but for all that, he is merely a dog. To suspect that he might have a human-like understanding of the proceedings around him would be ridiculous."

"Yes, I must agree it is quite absurd. But it, on the other hand, would be awfully exciting if we found in Julius Caesar such an exceptional dog! Do you not agree?" says Miss Elizabeth, looking up and smiling into my master's eyes.

"Yes, I agree," says my master softly, returning the smile with a smile.

I am certain that whether or not I am an exceptional dog is not the topmost thing on his mind now. I almost sense my master's body temperature goes up a degree. A sure sign that he wishes to repeat the heavenly experience of touching her sweet lips with his again.

An exceptional dog that I am, I immediately assess the situation, and again go off and make myself scarce to leave the lovers alone so that they will not feel inhibited by my presence.

* * * * *

We are visiting the Bennets at Longourn again today. My master and Miss Elizabeth have agreed that my master will ask Mr Bennet for permission to seek his daughter's hand in marriage today.

I am more than ordinarily curious to witness Mr Bennet's reaction to this unexpected turn of events, so I follow my master to Mr Bennet's library.

My master knocks on the door, and in hearing the voice 'Enter!' from within, opens the door and goes in, as I, too, slip through like a shadow after my master.

Mr Bennet raises his indolent eyes from his book, and seeing who the visitor is, looks uncommonly surprised.

"Why, Mr Darcy, this is most unprecedented," cries Mr Bennet. "And

Julius Caesar as well. I suppose you have come to show me how Julius Caesar's tail has been perfectly mended after that snare incident to set my mind at rest? It is very thoughtful of you."

"Julius Caesar is, indeed, absolutely fine now, and so he has been for a long time. The injury was not at all serious in the first place. But, sir, that is not why I am here thus at the risk of inconveniencing you," says my master. "I have come for far more important business."

Well! Far more important business than me! But I do not complain to be thus carelessly thrust aside, because I know my place. Of course, this matter at hand is by far the gravest moment in my master's life.

"Oh? That sounds rather ponderous," says Mr Bennet in a slightly apprehensive fashion. "I hope none of Mr Bingley's hounds have been caught in my gamekeeper's snares."

"Nothing of the sort, sir," says my master with a slight tilt of the mouth, which could barely be termed even an awry smile. "Erm ..." my master hesitates before he takes the plunge. "I have come, sir, to... to... to..." he stutters, uncharacteristically but understandably, "to ask for your p... permission," he stutters again, "to solicit M... M... M..." he stutters even for the third time, indicative of his nervous state, "Miss Elizabeth's hand in marriage."

Having managed to utter this much, my master lets out a long sigh, as if a heavy load had been taken off his shoulder.

The sheer unexpectedness of what he has just heard seems to have left Mr Bennet completely agape. He stares at my master for a good five seconds blankly, blinks a few times, then shakes his head rapidly a couple of times as if to whip himself out of a momentary distraction.

Then, "Eh?" says Mr Bennet rather absent-mindedly. "Did I hear you right? Or did I only fancy I heard it? Surely you cannot have said you wished to marry my daughter." Mr Bennet puts his ring finger in his ear and wiggles it a while, as if to make sure his ears are in proper working order.

My master smiles a wry smile again, and says, "You have not misheard me, sir. I did say I wished to be granted your daughter's hand in marriage. And I have to confess my culpability, sir. I have been so audacious as to solicit her hand before even asking you."

"And the fact that you are here to ask for my permission... Am I right to assume that Elizabeth accepted you, then?"

"Yes," says my master, "she has made me the happiest man upon earth."

"You have both of you kept the secret astoundingly well. I have never detected any particular partiality on either side. Who would have thought that you, Mr Darcy, were at all interested in women, least of all Lizzy. You always seemed so aloof, or, should I say, even frosty to any women. And if I may be frank, I am flabbergasted to hear Lizzy accepted you, as I always had this impression that, though she seemed to be awfully fond of Julius Caesar, she was not very fond of you, Mr Darcy," says Mr Bennet without mincing words.

"There you are correct, sir, at least up until quite recently," says my master truthfully without taking offence. "I cannot deny that Miss Elizabeth's sentiment towards me was not so much mere dislike as absolute abhorrence at one time. I will make a clean breast of it, sir. Last April, I asked her to be my wife, but was flatly rejected. But I should be the first one to admit that I well deserved to be. I was a repugnant, conceited fool. But there were some misunderstandings, too, and now all those have been cleared up, and I hope and trust that Miss Elizabeth's feelings for me have improved out of all recognition."

"Do you now? Well, if both of you are certain of your own feelings and it is what you really wish, I have no objection. I will give you blessings without reserve," says Mr Bennet.

And my master visibly heaves a sigh of relief.

* * * * *

My master is unsure what Mrs Bennet's reception of the news is to be. He is a little worried that she may not be best pleased with the prospect of having her hated man as her son-in-law. But I am more than certain there will be no objection from that quarter.

Mrs Bennet might not be the wisest of human beings, but she is not, deep down, a bad person. I am not saying this just because she has oftentimes shown unexpected kindness towards me. Of course, one tends to have a weakness for whoever may show kindness towards one and to speak of the person leniently, and I readily admit I have that weakness, but I think one can tell if someone is truly bad.

Being silly and being bad are two completely different things. It often happens that someone who possesses intelligence aplenty can be all the more villainous. Take Mr Wickham, for example. No one can say he is stupid, but the more intelligent a man of that sort is, the worse villain he is.

Mrs Bennet is silly and shallow, and can take offence easily. As it is often the case, however, someone like her, silly and simple but deep down not a bad soul, can forget offence easily, too.

Her hatred towards my master no doubt is a result of the offence my master carelessly caused by slighting her daughter Miss Elizabeth at the first meeting. So, mark my word. The offence will be cleanly forgotten as if it had never been, the moment that slight is rectified.

* * * * *

We are now gathered in the drawing room at Longbourn. I was absolutely right. Mrs Bennet's change of attitude towards my master is almost farcical, and she is now all solicitousness to my master.

But her acrimony thus fully abated, she seems, fortunately, to be somewhat awed by my master in exchange, and to my master's great relief, she does not treat him with that staggeringly noisy and hearty familiarity with which she treats her other son-in-law-to-be, Mr Bingley. But she obviously is fully mindful of seeing to every need and comfort of this new rather awe-inspiring future son-in-law of hers, and in a bid to delegate the task to her daughter, perpetually tells Miss Elizabeth to do this and to do that.

“Lizzy, dear,” says Mrs Bennet, “has Mr Darcy enough tea still left in his cup? Ask Mr Darcy.”

“Mama, I have already done so twice by your bidding and Mr Darcy's answer, on both occasions, was 'yes'.”

Chapter 20

"But Lizzy, that was more than one and a half minutes ago. And in any event, Mr Darcy might have only been reticent. And what about cakes and biscuits? And oh, yes, the cucumber sandwiches! They have turned out uncommonly well today, and they, I believe, are Mr Darcy's favourite. Offer them to Mr Darcy, Lizzy!"

Miss Elizabeth, knowing her mother well, apparently judges it better to comply with her, and letting out a small sigh, asks my master in her charming and jocular manner which my master is a total slave to, "Mr Darcy, would you like another cup of tea, and may I offer you some more sandwiches? Or are the cakes and sandwiches swimming in your stomach?"

My master's stomach, I would have thought, would by now be filled to saturation with tea as he has already imbibed no less than five cups of the beverage to humour his future mother-in-law. But he seems, nevertheless, unable to say 'no' again to Miss Elizabeth. Meeting her mischievous smile with a rare laughter, he says, "Yes, please, thank you."

Whether or not to show her sincere solicitousness to my master, Mrs Bennet also raises her level of kindness to me today. As she will perpetually bid Miss Elizabeth tend to my master's needs and comforts, so will she perpetually tend to mine herself. She will not leave me alone. She continuously tries to feed me, for which honour I am most sensible, but I am sure too much food is not good for me. I know we dogs are the healthiest when we eat only once a day, or twice at the oftenest. And moreover, Mrs Bennet is very much the mother of her two youngest daughters', in that she noisily hugs and squeezes me, and ruffles my hair till it is rumpled up into an undignified mess. But a stoical dog that I am, I gladly take the indignity for my master's sake.

Chapter 20

Chapter 21

In which the two happy couples tie the knot

It has been decided that the two happy couples will have a double wedding at the parish church of St Martin's.

"Oh, how envious of me every mama in the neighbourhood will be! They will indeed!" says Mrs Bennet excitedly. "Gaining two such sons-in-law at once! Oh, how happy I shall be watching you two fine gentlemen stand at the altar with the two dearest of my daughters! I shall perish with the sheer excitement and bliss! I shall indeed! And then, after the ceremony, we will hold a wedding-feast at Longbourn!"

"But, Mrs Bennet," interrupts Mr Bingley tentatively, "will it not be more convenient to have the wedding-dinner at Netherfield?"

"It is according to the tradition to have it at the bride's place. And beside, there are two brides in this case, so it should be even more so," insists Mrs Bennet.

"But, Mama, I have never heard that such is the tradition," protests Miss Bennet.

"It is a tradition," insists Mrs Bennet more doggedly. "What would you know? You have not lived long enough to have heard of it, or to know anything for that matter."

"But as Mr Bingley says," Miss Bennet persists, going against her mother's words with unusual firmness, "tradition or no tradition, it will be more convenient to have the wedding-feast at Netherfield, surely, for Netherfield is far nearer to St Martin's, and people will be able to park their carriages at Netherfield and can just walk over to the church, if they wish, and from the church to Netherfield after the ceremony."

"Moreover, Mama," interjects Miss Elizabeth in aid of her sister, "as we have agreed, most of the relatives and friends will be staying at Netherfield, and so they would find it far more congenial if they do not have to travel from Longbourn to Netherfield after the feast. You know what people are like after a hearty libation. It stands to reason that we have the wedding-feast at Netherfield."

"Well, if you put it that way, you may be right," concedes Mrs Bennet begrudgingly.

So, Mrs Bennet finally agrees that, all things considered, the wedding-dinner at Netherfield might be a more viable option.

* * * * *

My master has written to Miss Darcy at Pemberley, imparting to her the happy tidings, and at the same time asking her to make haste to come and join the rest at Netherfield to be at the wedding.

Mr Bingley, too, seems to have dispatched a missive to Scarborough, where the Hursts and Miss Bingley still are, notifying them of the upcoming happy event, viz, the double wedding, and asking them to travel south to attend the wedding. They will not be best pleased with their brother's choice, and will be gnashing their teeth, finding their effort of last November to separate their brother from the offending family has come to nothing.

But that aside, what will Miss Bingley's reaction be when she finds that her hopes are dashed thus at one fell swoop and my master has become inexorably beyond her reach?

Chapter 21

* * * * *

Lady Catherine de Bourgh is not amused, or to be more precise, she seems to have flown into a wild rage. According to my master, she has written to him in the foulest language imaginable, employing a string of vocabulary which he says should not have come from any lady of quality. She has used such colourful language, my master puts it, as would have made even a fishwife blush at. What kind of language can that possibly be? I would love to know. But disappointingly, my master does not elaborate upon it. Judging, however, from the much aggrieved, profuse way my master is muttering and disparaging his aunt, Lady Catherine must have lashed out a barrage of insults at his beloved Miss Elizabeth. Lady Catherine, methinks, has made a fatal mistake. If his aunt had insulted him, and him alone, my master might have tolerated it, but his dearly beloved being insulted with some defiling language! Goodness gracious! He will not be easily mollified. It will be a very long time before the offence can be forgiven.

I anticipate a long-term rift between the aunt and the nephew, and the prospect, if I may say so, is a perfectly congenial one to me.

* * * * *

Miss Darcy is come from Pemberley to attend the wedding. As I fully anticipated, her joy for the prospect of gaining Miss Elizabeth as her sister is heartfelt and genuine. Miss Darcy took a great liking to Miss Elizabeth the very first moment they met at Pemberley back in August, and showed it as openly as her extremely retiring nature allowed. And now, as she talks to Miss Elizabeth, her face absolutely blooms into a blissful smile as its colour heightened, and my master is observing his two most beloved ladies with joyous contentment.

Contrary to the blissful expressions upon Miss Darcy's face, those upon Mr Bingley's sisters' are anything but blissful, but at least Mrs Hurst appears to be trying her hardest to be civil to the two wives-to-be, Miss Bennet and Miss Elizabeth.

Chapter 21

* * * * *

I pass by the bedchamber belonging to Miss Bingley, where it seems Miss Bingley and Mrs Hurst are at the moment confabulating.

"Caroline, let me give you a word of advice" I hear Mrs Hurst say to her sister. "I know exactly how you are feeling, and what it takes to accept your defeat. It must be very hard when reality comes crushing down. And to behave cordially towards Miss Eliza must be the last thing you wish to be asked to do at the moment, but you should restrain yourself more. Now that the nuptials are firmly to take place, we cannot do anything about it. It is not as if we could turn the clock back. And at any event, we did what we could to draw Mr Darcy's interest in your direction, but it was not to be, and so, you have to withdraw graciously."

I am surprised that Mrs Hurst can be so sensible. Miss Bingley maintains a sullen silence.

"And it was, I dare say,," adds Mrs Hurst, "in no little part your own fault, Caroline."

"What do you mean by that, Louisa? How can it have been my fault?" demands Miss Bingley.

"You should have studied Mr Darcy's predilections a little harder," explains Mrs Hurst a little pedantically, "taking lessons from Miss Eliza's clever ways."

"Oh, how could I?" protests Miss Bingley. "I do not have Miss Eliza's honed skill at cunning! I am by nature exceedingly honest. As straight as a die as anyone would agree. I could not possibly have lowered myself to employ any artifice. Such would have been totally against my character!"

"Oh, I know you are honest, as am I, and indeed, it would have been difficult for you to resort to any dissimulation, as it would have been for me, too. But sometimes, in affairs of love and courtship, it is necessary to be a little dishonest and artful, as I, too, was often told when I was younger and was being courted."

Chapter 21

I am struck dumb with astoundment. How Miss Bingley and Mrs Hurst can call themselves honest and free of cunning with straight faces is utterly beyond me.

"But that aside, what I wish to say to you here, Caroline," Mrs Hurst continues, "is that you should lay aside the chagrin and try to be a little more civil to Miss Eliza. Men, once they are married, will go to a great length to humour their wives, and listen to whatever their beloved wives say. Hurst is exactly so, as you might have noticed. He would do anything I say. And impressive and formidable as Mr Darcy may seem, he will be just the same. If you continue your present attitude and Miss Eliza takes umbrage at your behaviour, she might wish to exclude you from Pemberley and exercise her will. Then, Mr Darcy will be sure to acquiesce, whether or not you are his best friend's sister. You, Caroline, do not wish to be barred from Pemberley, I presume?"

"Of course not!" says Miss Bingley snappishly.

"Then you should curb your acrimony towards Miss Eliza. Moreover, if you continue in the present wise and incur Miss Eliza's ire, even I, as your sister, might also come to be barred from Pemberley by association, and I do not wish that to happen. Surely, Caroline, you do not wish to place your dear sister in such a predicament, either, do you?"

I thought Mrs Hurst had become unusually sensible and decided to admonish her little sister of her unwise behaviour for her sister's sake, but I should have known better. She is merely doing so for fear that Pemberley society should become out of bounds for her herself.

"Oh, well. I know what you say makes sense," thus concedes Miss Bingley in the end. "It certainly is useless to hanker after what is not to be. As you say, I do not wish the gates of Pemberley to be barred against me. And in any event, it is not as if Mr Darcy were the only fish in the sea."

"Exactly. So, instead of falling into the mopes over an escaped fish, you would do far better to reflect upon your past mistakes and prepare yourself for the next catch."

Chapter 21

"You are absolutely right. Well, I shall try to behave more cordially towards Miss Eliza from now on. After all I only have to pretend. I do not really have to try to like her, do I?"

"Precisely so," says the sagacious sister.

* * * * *

The banns have been read for three Sundays, and today is the impatiently anticipated wedding day.

Being the exceptionally well behaved canine companion that I am, I should, methinks, be allowed to accompany my master and sit next to him in the front pew in the church and watch the wedding ceremony proceed. But that may be too much to hope for.

But at least I should be able to sneak into the church after someone and go and find an obscure corner somewhere. I am, if I may say so myself, rather expert at making myself very unobtrusive. That is naturally a necessary skill as a gun dog. How else can we gun dogs stalk birds without alerting them?

* * * * *

Now, people are gathered in the church, waiting for the brides to arrive. I secrete myself on some sort of dais in the dark, hidden corner behind one of the pillars near the North Transept.

Judging that ladies are more unlikely than gentlemen to notice me sneaking past, being too absorbed in confabulating to pay attention to a mere dog, I chose the time to sneak in when a congregation of ladies stood on the porch busily exchanging greetings and gossips. And thus, I successfully stole an entry into the church. I, then, skulked towards the front of the church, hugging the shadows of the walls so as not to draw attention to myself, and finally stationed myself in this position which is well sequestered but still affords me a tolerable view of the congregation.

The bridegrooms are there in the front pew, and I watch them while they sit next to each other, flanked by their respective groomsmen,

Colonel Fitzwilliam and Mr Bingley's first cousin, Mr Theodolphus Bingley.

Among the low hum of people's whisperings, I cannot detect my master's heartbeats, or Mr Bingley's, but I am more than certain that their hearts are beating loudly, lub dub, lub dub, lub dub ...

My master looks a little nervous, but the aura that surrounds him now is far more happy than nervous. His mouth is touched by a faint smile and his eyes are dreamy and seem to reflect nothing but happiness and hope for the future. I suppose Mr Bingley at a glance might look the more openly happy, my master being far less demonstrative. But I think that, because my master normally very seldom smiles, the impact of his smiles when he does is far more potent than Mr Bingley's, as I have often heard ladies say.

Among the faces in the church, I seek one particular face – Miss Bingley's. As I thought, her face is not smiling. Hers probably is the only face in this congregation not smiling. Even Mrs Hurst's is. I am not fond of Miss Bingley, as I might have often mentioned, but even I feel a little sorry for her now. I bethink myself what it must feel like to have to witness your loved one come irrevocably to belong to someone else. It must be truly heart-rending. Indeed, I would not wish it even upon my worst enemy. But on second thoughts ... Does Miss Bingley's love for my master, I wonder, really merit such sympathy? Does she really love my master with the sincere ardency of an innocent maiden? I rather suspect it is not the case. Is it, I wonder, more like a craving for a trophy or a prize? And of rather a mercenary kind? Then, as I overhead her say to her sister, once that trophy is gone, she will begin chasing after another prize in no time.

Well, in any event, now is not the time to be wasting my thoughts upon the likes of Miss Bingley.

The sound of a carriage is perceived to stop outside in front of the church. The brides must have arrived. The priest gestures the bridegrooms to rise and stand in front of him.

A hush descends upon the crowd as they hear the apparent sound of the door opening and the brides entering the church. They turn round and crane their necks to catch sight of the brides. And then, they let out a huge, collective sigh of admiration as they at last see the beautiful brides halt at the far end of the nave before commencing their stately approach to the altar.

Of course, I have always thought those two eldest Misses Bennets uncommonly beautiful, but as I behold them now, the vision they project, clad in virginal white gowns, is almost out of this world.

Now, they walk up the aisle, each holding the proud father's arm. They now and then answer to people's admiring smiles and approving nods, Miss Bennet with shy blushes and Miss Elizabeth with brilliant smiles.

When they are nearing the bridegrooms who stand facing the priest, Miss Elizabeth espies me peering at her from my dark hiding place, and gives me a somewhat conspiratorial secret smile. Has she divined immediately that I gained a clandestine *entrée* into the church? A lady of awesomely quick parts that she is, I would not be at all surprised if she had.

The brides finally stand next to their respective bridegrooms, and then, and only then, the bridegrooms turn their heads and look at the brides.

Oh! The expression upon my master's face when he beholds his beloved Miss Elizabeth! Deep love, elation, yearning, happiness ... One can see there all the emotions one would expect to see in the face of a man who is experiencing consummate beatitude!

My heart is full. My vision would certainly have dimmed here, were I a human being. I do not wish to boast, and I by no means intend to suggest that I am the architect of all this, or to claim all the glory of bringing my master and Miss Elizabeth together. But I might at least be allowed to say that I have played some important part in their union.

Chapter 21

Chapter 22

In which, the inquisitive dog that I am, I eavesdrop on the happy couple in their most intimate moments in their bedchamber

We left Netherfield after the wedding feast yesterday afternoon. It is now mid-afternoon, and my master and my mistress have just arrived at Pemberley after stopping overnight upon the way. The journey north from Hertfordshire has been fairly swift and comfortable.

Mr Meadows, my master's butler, and Mrs Reynolds, my master's housekeeper at Pemberley, welcome their master and their new mistress with genuine gladness. Of course, they met Mrs Darcy in August, and the perspicacious people that they are, they seem to have divined my master's deep love for the lady even then, and I think this marriage has not at all come as a surprise for them.

* * * * *

My master and my mistress refreshed themselves after the journey and have just partaken of some light collation to fill their stomachs.

Mrs Darcy expresses her desire to stroll for a while in the grounds of

Pemberley to avoid postprandial lassitude.

"It is not good for one's health," says Mrs Darcy, "to stand idle after meals. One ought to stay always energetic."

My mistress, of course, is not one of those ladies of the *ton* who consider that the air of ennui is an essential part of being fashionable.

"Are you sure you are not too fatigued after the journey?" asks my master.

"Oh, yes, of course I am sure. You made sure the journey was comfortable and not too exhausting for me. I am not tired in the least," replies Mrs Darcy.

And so, my master with pleasure offers to be her guide. And I accompany them as a matter of course.

"Last time I was here," says Mrs Darcy, "I regretted that I was not able to enjoy these beautiful parks to my heart's content, as my aunt was not a very good walker. That time, who would have imagined that I would someday be enjoying the walks as one who actually belongs to this place!"

"I hope that was not the only regret you left behind then when you were compelled to leave Derbyshire so suddenly?" says my master a little jocularly, with a tender smile at his new beloved wife,

Mrs Darcy, with a mischievous glint in her eyes, says, "Oh, of course not! I was immensely loath to part with Julius Caesar!"

My master laughs at that, and says, "Oh, yes, Julius Caesar, of course! But what about his master? Were you loath to part with him, too, Elizabeth? Even a little?"

Mrs Darcy smiles a somewhat timorous smile, turns to face my master, and toying with my master's neckcloth in a most uncharacteristic, shy and missish fashion totally unlike her normal self, says, "Yes, I was very loath to part from him. But at that time I was fearful, or rather, convinced that Lydia's infamy and my family's disgrace would make him wish never to see me again, and I regretted my former folly bitterly which had prevented me from seeing the real goodness in him. I was profoundly sorrowful that I might never be able to see him again. But I felt I had paid dearly but deservedly for my folly, and was determined to hug the secret of my heart silently to myself."

"Oh, Elizabeth!" cries my master as if his emotions has got the better of him, and gathering his beloved into his arms, presses her to his bosom tightly and kisses her with an unprecedented ardency.

I, suppressing my desire to stare and gawp at them, assume a perfect nonchalance as usual for fear of making them feel self-conscious.

* * * * *

My master, a consummate pattern of the supremely adoring, considerate husband that he is, wished to give his new bride an unforgettable, sublime memory of their first conjugal union in the beautiful bedroom at Pemberley, and refrained, in spite of his mounting desire, from suffering Mrs Darcy the rigours of the first experience of the marital intimacy on the night spent in the hostelry on the journey north.

So, if I might be allowed to be so forward as to say such a thing, this night is to be the very first night of their nuptial intimacy.

Oh, I feel so excited for my master! I am not being nosy or anything, but I am all agog to know how my master will proceed with it.

Of course, such activities are far from new to my master. He is as experienced, if not more, in such things as any virile young gentlemen of the *ton* of his age would be – that is, the ripe age of twenty-eight. He has had quite a few encounters of the sort, though none, I must stress firmly, with an innocent. Decent gentlemen with strong principles never even dream of dallying with innocents, as that unprincipled villain, Mr Wickham, has frequently done with the sole motive of despoiling them of their virtue simply for his carnal satisfaction with no thoughts whatsoever for the maidens' reputation or future.

So, anyway, my master will know exactly what to do.

* * * * *

Chapter 22

With the curtain of nightfall, I have stolen into the suite of rooms which newly belongs to my master and my mistress. This is the principal bedchamber suite. Two sumptuous bed-chambers next to each other linked by a connecting door, each bedchamber with a dressing room and another room, my master's with a study and my mistress's with a boudoir. I go and jump up onto the window seat and hide myself behind the drawn curtains.

You might think my conduct utterly out of order and strongly object to my taking such egregious liberty. And it goes, I cannot deny, somewhat against the grain for me, too. But as the chronicler of this history, I consider it my sacred duty to depict the moments which are to be the most important, the most beautiful, and the most glorious of my master's life.

Oh, I hear my master and my mistress just outside my mistress's bedchamber door!

"Then, I shall leave you here," I hear my master say. "I trust your maid will be already waiting to help you with the night toilet. I shall be with you in an hour or so."

I hear my mistress answer with a shy and a little tremulous 'Yes', and I can almost see her flushed face. Vivacious and plucky as she may be in normal circumstances, Mrs Darcy, after all, is still an untouched *ingénue*. She must be feeling ever so nervous about the night ahead.

I hear my mistress's door open and then shut, denoting that she has gone into her own chamber. Oh, and now my master has come into his own! I bate my breath and ready myself to pretend to be asleep if necessary in the unlikely event that my master happens to open the window curtains.

Hmm ... He seems to have gone into his dressing room, where Mr Trent is waiting to help him prepare for the night. Soon, I hear the sound of my master performing his ablutions, and later on, of Mr Trent preparing for my master's night toilet and the low hum of their voices ...

Thus, I wait patiently for my master to finish his night toilet for a good half hour more. Then, at last, I hear Mr Trent leaving.

This is it! I again bate my breath, and listen. My master's footsteps cross the room to the connecting door to my mistress's room. If I said my master walks purposefully with a spring in his steps, I would not be at all exaggerating. Then, my master knocks softly but rapidly twice, at which a soft, bashful 'Yes' is heard from the other side of the door. And I almost hear my master' heartbeat suddenly quicken out of proportion. He opens the door.

I gingerly peek out of the chink of the curtains. Most fortunately, this side of the connecting door, namely, my master's room, is lit very dimly now, only one candle burning upon the mantelpiece. My mistress's room is less dim, but only marginally. I am sure her maidenly modesty has made her shy away from being in a brightly lit room with my master.

My master goes into the room. Oh, I cannot believe my luck! He has left the door open!

My master walks up to his wife, and stops only about a foot away from her. From where I am peeping, my mistress's form is just about visible to me. Though there is some hint of trepidation and shyness in the way she holds herself, I do not see any sign that she is feeling apprehensive about the so-far unknown world she is soon to be plunged into. What I can see in her upturned face is a total trust in her husband, the belief that he will never hurt her. I hope my master will be able to act deservedly for that trust, will be able to curb his enthusiasm and take it slow and easy for his beloved's sake. Otherwise, he might frighten the living daylights out of her.

Her eyes looks huge and luminous, and her lips are a little parted, in what people often call 'a very inviting way', a kind of look that would make any male with hot blood wild with desire. Not that I have experienced such an emotion myself at first hand, but I have heard it mentioned countless times and, if I be honest, even happened upon scenes of such a nature a few times.

My master gathers his wife into his arms in a very tender caress, suggesting, to my great relief, that he has at least some self-possession not to rush precipitately into making violent love to her. He, then, murmurs sweet nothings to her ear, softly kissing her and stroking her, presumably to make her feel at ease, and, if I may be so bold as to suggest such a thing, to arouse her.

Yes, my master is quite an old hand at this. No greenhorn in the art of lovemaking, methinks, could ever behave so collectedly with the svelte form of the love of his life clad only in a flimsy nightdress clasped in his arms.

After some time, my master sweeps my mistress up into his arms and disappears from my sight. I presume he is carrying her to the bed, which, to my regret, cannot be seen from my hiding place.

I listen carefully.

I sneak out of my hiding place, taking great care not to make any noise. I first go and position myself behind the wall by the side of the open doorway, and carefully poke my head out to assess how the situation lies. I debate whether or not I should take my position under the bed. If I go under the bed, I will not be able to see them. But on the other hand, if I take position where I can command a good view of them, the reverse will be true, too, and they will also be able to see me if they happen to look around. But will I be content just to be able to hear them. Probably not? I crane my neck into the room to see if there is anything which would help me conceal myself effectively. Lo! Just the thing! I see a screen in one corner, whose purpose presumably is to hide the offending chamberpot away from the eye.

Convinced that my master, let alone my mistress, is by now much too preoccupied with their own proceedings to pay attention to what might be going on around them, I take a stealthy step into the room. I work my way towards the screen, and thus, manage safely to station myself behind it. It is a four-panelled screen, and there are three fissures where the panels meet. These three fissures are all fairly conveniently angled, but I find the one in the middle especially well placed.

I peer out of the fissure.

Chapter 22

I see my master has placed his dear wife upon the bed. And lying propped up on his elbow, he is tenderly caressing her and kissing her. Oh, what a beautiful picture it is! There is nothing more beautiful than the image of two people deeply in love in the act of loving.

My master certainly knows how to arouse a woman, how to make her crave for more. The rhythm and the quality of my mistress's breathing gradually change, and soon it is apparent she is feeling it a great deal. And then, my master considers the time has come for them to be finally united in the true sense.

"Elizabeth, my dear love," says my master, "this might hurt, but do not be afraid. Please bear with it just a while for me."

"I am not afraid," my mistress says. "How can I be afraid of whatever you do out of your love for me?"

"Oh, Elizabeth!" he says, and kisses her again, and then, forges ahead. My mistress gives a sound like a small whimper as if she is indeed in some sudden pain.

"Oh, my love!" cries my master hotly against her lips. "Forgive me! I have given you pain! But you will be comfortable in a while, I promise. Relax, and take a deep breath."

And my mistress seems to do as she is told.

"Are you a little more comfortable now?" my master asks, and in reply to that, my mistress twines her arms around his neck as if to ask for more.

My master must be nearly at his limits, his beloved thus tight around him. But still, he seems to decide it is too soon to make violent love to her yet. So instead, he endeavours to proceed as slowly and with as much tender care as he is able under the circumstances.

His care seems to take effect by and by, and the pain clearly is in time forgotten.

"Ah ..." my mistress lets out a moan, but then, she seems to feel suddenly self-conscious, and tries to suppress her voice in maidenly embarrassment.

"Do not try to suppress your voice," says my master. "Let me hear it. Your voice is music to my ear. Let loose the heavenly music which is a natural expression of how you are feeling."

My master certainly knows what to say.

I have once or twice overheard some gentlemen saying in their rather bawdy conversations that it is very unlikely that a man can bring an innocent to her release at her first time.

But my master's skill and care seems to work wonders, as my mistress no doubt is now reaching the height of ecstasy. She clings to my master ever so tightly, her nails almost digging into my master's back, as she reaches her release. And then, my master joins her in his own completion, muttering to her, "Oh, Elizabeth, Elizabeth, my love! My life!"

* * * * *

I can hear their soft slow regular breathing now, and know that they are now in deep, contented sleep.

And I shall now leave the happy couple thus at their happiest moment.

Finis

Chapter 22

Made in the USA
Lexington, KY
07 December 2014